JUST A WHISPER

SHEILA WILSON

WESTBOW
PRESS®
A DIVISION OF THOMAS NELSON
& ZONDERVAN

Scripture taken from the King James Version of the Bible.

WestBow Press books may be ordered through booksellers or by contacting:

WestBow Press
A Division of Thomas Nelson & Zondervan
1663 Liberty Drive
Bloomington, IN 47403
www.westbowpress.com
1 (866) 928-1240

ISBN: 978-1-9736-2216-1 (sc)
ISBN: 978-1-9736-2215-4 (e)

Print information available on the last page.

WestBow Press rev. date: 03/02/2018

Dedication:

To my husband (David) and daughter (Callie) who embody love and acceptance of people from all walks of life.

A Whisper

Just a whisper defeated our King
Crushed and bruised him relentlessly
This whisper said with a careless fling
Then it grew and grew to Calvary

This whisper repeated with no thought or care
of who it would hurt or where it would go
This whisper caused such terrible pain.
Did the one who began this really know?

This whisper ambled from town to town.
Up through the mountains
and grew with a swell.
How could it cause such a feverish sound?
While Satan laughed from the pits of hell.

I saw the blood and I saw the pain
as he hung upon the tree.
Then my tears came as falling rain,
for this whisper began with me!

I clung to the cross and wept to my Lord
Please forgive me for I never knew.
He gently looked at this wretched soul
and softly whispered, "I Love You!"

CONTENTS

FOREWORD

In my twenty seventh year, I finally humbled myself and found "The Christ" which I had rejected in my youth. After dabbling in many different avenues and religions to fill this hole in my soul, God put in my path a couple who were not afraid or embarrassed to love me to redemption. They handed me a bible and told me to never lie to God. I took this advice to heart and started my journey.

I began reading the bible from front to back. The first time I read it, Jehovah sent me on a journey with my senses. The fragrances of The Garden of Eden were heavenly, the sorrow of Abraham in being instructed to sacrifice his favored son brought me to tears, the parting of the Red Sea made me gasp in wonder and the crucifixion of "The Christ" horrified, devastated, perplexed and angered me for days.

On my second journey through the scriptures, from front to back, questions began formulating in my mind. I would go to church and ask these questions. Some were answered and sometimes I was just looked at like I was weird. Sincere statements I made began to be refuted and mocked in the pulpit. One lovely lady even admonished me that there were some things you just didn't talk about in church. It was then I realized the people in the church are flawed and imperfect even after knowing "The Christ". A great love for this congregation grew in me and continues to this day. I could have taken offense, but instead God took these experiences to lead me to different ways to get my answers. Jehovah always knows best.

My biggest question was, "What did this Jesus do that was so bad to warrant being crucified?" Even though you blindly believe in his perfection at the moment of conversion, it is not a sin to ask honest, heartfelt questions to this holy God. Sometimes he answers, sometimes he leads you down a road to discover your own answer and sometimes he just tells you it is none of your business. He is the Professor of all Professors!

The resulting story is a combination of journaling about life experiences and reading his word. At the end of a study of Mark, I realized how my journal fit together with this gospel. So I combined them in a fictional account inspired by the real account of Jesus Christ. I laid the manuscript aside until my mother came to see me one day. I told her about the manuscript and what I had learned through writing it and how wicked the tongue can be. She looked me in the eye, standing at the back door, with sunlight streaming on her face and said, "You're right, with just a whisper you can cause a person's destruction."

CHAPTER 1

The young man who walked to the Jordan River that morning was not outstanding in physique or dress, yet there was a tingle in the air as he passed people on the road. Eyes were drawn to him as he neared them. Some looked away as he passed by while others pondered in their hearts why this man had such a profound effect upon them without even speaking a word. John was baptizing people that day and though he had been prophesying about the need for repentance and the savior's appearing, even he was not prepared for the wonder he was to encounter. Yahweh prepares us and then pleasantly surprises us with his timing or presence at a time we least expect it. People seem to find this out when they look inwardly rather than outwardly for change in their circumstances.

The man walked slowly to where John stood waist deep in water calling for the repentance of sin. He humbly approached John and when John saw him it was as if the world stood still. John instantly knew who this unremarkable man was and bowed his head as his knees buckled. He had grown up with him, even recognizing him when he was in the womb. Yet he had not pinpointed him as the Messiah he was looking for in all of his days of searching. Do we overlook a person who will create great change because they don't measure up to the list of attributes we have humanly foisted upon them? Do we miss out on seeing God's hand move because a person does not meet the criteria humanity has set up for success?

John now recognized him as the Messiah, the one Jehovah had

promised. His body became weak with the realization of whose presence he was in.

Then joy lifted him as he told the crowds, *"Look! There is the Lamb of God who takes away the world's sin! He is the one I was talking about when Isaiah said a man far greater than I am is coming, who existed long before me! I didn't know he was the one, but I am here baptizing with water in order to point him out to the nation of Israel."*

As John placed his hand on Jesus' shoulder the magnitude of his mission became clear. A torrent of emotions flooded John's whole being causing him to hesitate. Feeling unworthy, John told Jesus, "This isn't proper. I am the one who needs to be baptized by you." Jesus steadfastly looked at John and replied, *"Let it be so now, for thus it is fitting for us to fulfill all righteousness."*

Suddenly his emotions were calmed and the strength returned to John's body and he relented. He baptized the young man in the Jordan River, knowing he was witnessing the beginning of a ministry which would change the world. People, crowded around the banks of the Jordan River, watched as John and the young man spoke with each other, unaware they were beholding a scene which would be recorded in the greatest book ever written. If they had known, would things have been different or would they have rushed to crush the young man right there in the river? We will never know for only God could see inside the minds and hearts of the crowd. He had chosen this time, this fullness of time.

As Jesus arose from the cool, gentle waters, the heavens opened up and the spirit of God descended upon him in the form of a dove. A voice from heaven said, "You are my beloved son, in whom I am well pleased." The crowd looked above as the rumble from the skies resounded across the sky. Their ears were so full of their own words, they could not discern the words of the one whom they had longed to hear from for so long. Their lives were shackled by rules, regulations, laws which were beginning to crush them. They yearned for these chains to be lifted as they continued to follow the rituals put on them by

Jewish authority hoping to attain the attention of God. Yet if they had heard would history be different or would it be even crueler?

The gentle man immediately left the Jordan River disappearing in the direction of the wilderness. Many people were concerned that the young man had become disoriented because of the emotional moment of baptism, yet they made no attempt to stop him or give guidance. Some people laughed at the man for going the wrong way, saying he must be deranged. Other people did not even notice because they were so caught up in their own little world of self importance.

One group watching the scene was a small group of women. They stood in the back of the crowd so they could survey who was there, how they acted, what they wore, and what they said. They had a habit of taking what they saw and heard in life and changing it to ridicule, denigrate, or even destroy people. It was a game to them and saw no harm in it. They were only words and words could not cut or curtail a person's life, right?

These women would start the ember which would create the blaze that changed the world. If they had known then, would they have raced home to be with their loved ones or continued on with their wicked tongues? Only God the Father knows.

The women were there because of the crowds and commotion. They loved to be in the center of activity so they could learn firsthand what was happening in their region. These women would not wait for their husbands' return home. They felt their husbands left out the best parts. The juicy, tantalizing parts which made them feel superior and above the common stock. They were women who had been blessed with family, money, power in their speech, standing in the community, and a need for control in their surroundings.

As they watched the rough, stocky man called John preach to the crowds about repentance, their thoughts were not on the message, but the messenger. They had heard of this man who lived in the desert and kept to himself. He was an odd sort of fellow, really not worthy of their notice. For some unknown reason he had left the isolation of the desert and become some type of prophet. He traveled around the country telling of the coming of the promised Messiah and calling for repentance. There were many men of this caliber and they eventually went on into oblivion. There was only one difference at this time and the leader of the group of women took note of it.

Now he had identified this scraggly, young man of lowly birth to be the Savior for whom the Jews had been waiting. Surely John must be delirious or drunk. The long years of isolation in the desert had caused him to lose all reason. He just couldn't point out anyone he wanted and put the label of such high renown upon them. This is heresy!

Tracilla, wife of Micah, was a member of the priest tribe of the Jews, a descendant of Aaron. She was considered the leader of this small group of women. She thought of herself as superior to the majority of Jews. She wore the finest clothes and was continuously speaking about the wealth and position of her family. She was a tall, regal woman who had not been blessed with the beauty of face from her ancestors, which the holy manuscripts took note of. Her husband worked hard to provide for her every want and these multiplied daily. She spoke with authority and used this gift to deceive and manipulate people's thoughts and actions. She was very good at this and many people fell under her deceptive spirit. Many others followed and agreed with her because they did not want to be the recipient of her razor-like tongue. Control was behind every word or deed made by Tracilla. Mercy was not in her vocabulary when someone dare to confront or correct her.

At the river Tracilla was surrounded by her flock of eager and some reluctant minions. When she witnessed John pointing to the ignoble man as the Messiah, anger filled her already tainted heart. A darkness overcame Tracilla at that moment which would prove to be her undoing in the end. With this darkness, a strange sense of prideful, religious fever seem to emanate from it. She liked the feeling of it. It made her feel important and with purpose, something she was always seeking in her life. This darkness seemed to fill the empty void inside of her. A void she would not dare speak of as it would show her to be vulnerable or incomplete. A void she had attempted to fill with maliciousness, gossip, and manipulation. This darkness seemed to soothe the pain of emptiness.

If John were correct and this man is the Messiah, then all of her spoutings were false. Tracilla had always maintained the Messiah would be of the highest birth. His wealth and power would overshadow the earth and only the upper crust of the Jewish race would be saved by him. He would not bother with the lowly, poor, or simple people. Tracilla had always imagined her husband being the right hand man of the Messiah with her pulling the strings behind a curtain controlling the world. This vision in her mind gave her great joy and contentment. This darkness seemed to reassure her that this could happen if she would just fall into and be engulfed by its presence.

So Tracilla could not have such an ordinary man being recognized as the Holy One. This would expose her as being stupid, shallow, and powerless. This was something she could not and would not bear. As she watched the scene unfold before her, a plan hatched in her evil, little mind. It was as if an invisible force was feeding her thoughts causing her to feel she was invincible.

After the young man left the river, Tracilla put into motion her wicked plot. With her sweetest smile and empathetic expression, she looked at the people standing around her and said in a conspiratorial whisper, "That cannot be! We all know who that young man is. He is the son of Joseph and Mary of Nazareth. Joseph was a carpenter and Mary is a woman of simple means. Do you really think God would choose her to give birth to the King of Jews? The only thing in her life is caring for her family and I even recall there being a scandal with her engagement to Joseph. Everyone tried to keep it hush, hush, but we all know sin cannot be covered up. Our great Messiah would never come from such a lowly birth." The women were now clustered around Tracilla as she spoke. Tracilla had learned that the lower she spoke, the more apt people were to draw closer and in turn listen more attentively. So now the women were drawn into her circle of deception.

They were like lapdogs waiting for their next morsel of nourishment. They were not disappointed but the mantel of mind manipulation was on another member of the group.

Patisha, a short and portly lady, wanting to gain approval, readily agreed, "Yes, I remember hearing something about the scandal. It was truly shocking and her poor family suffered greatly because of her indiscretion. Fortunately for Mary, Joseph was a compassionate man and decided to hide her shame by not breaking their engagement." Patisha smiled very smugly as Tracilla looked on her with obvious approval.

Fueled by Tracilla's apparent acceptance of her tales, Patisha continued on with her story, "I can also tell you of a time when we traveled to Jerusalem for the annual passover and Mary lost her child on the journey home. We had been traveling a whole day before she discovered he was missing. Now, what kind of mother loses her child like that? Tracilla is being much too kind about the woman Mary when she says she cares so much for her family. She is really just a selfish, self absorbed simpleton whose sins have been conveniently covered up by the righteousness of others." With this Patisha raised her head proudly and seemed to bow to Tracilla.

Patisha had conveniently forgotten to mention that she herself had lost a child for three days during the wheat threshing. She had been so involved in one of Tracilla's gatherings she had even been reluctant to leave when her maidservant had come to deliver the news. The child had eventually been found safe and unharmed with Patisha blaming everyone else but herself. Patisha's memory was not the only weak character trait she possessed. She continued on embellishing her story of Mary's missing child adding fallacious details to titillate her friends' minds.

These remarks found their way into the hearts and minds of many people that day. When these people went home, the stories were changed, stretched, and distorted to absurd lengths. The spark was lit and people's imaginations blew it until it became a small fire. Tracilla and Patisha could have quickly stomped it out but they chose not to. Later they would regret not having taken the time to do so.

CHAPTER 2

After Jesus left the Jordan River he went into the wilderness. While he was there he was tempted by Satan in every way imaginable, yet he did not succumb. After every temptation he became stronger and more compassionate toward people. He had to experience firsthand what people went through in their daily fight with temptation and the deceiver's ploys.

Satan was relentless in his attack at the Savior, trying to make him fail, knowing his own failure would unleash on the earth an unbreakable bond offered to mankind to Jehovah God. We will never know everything Jesus went through until we reach the heavenly shore, yet he persevered for each individual born or to be born. This Christ loved us so much he wanted us to know he had walked in our shoes, shed the same tears, fought the same battles, and understood why we failed.

During this time Tracilla had almost forgotten about the young man. No one had seen or heard from him since the baptism at the Jordan River. She turned her attention to a new victim for her maliciousness.

A couple from Galilee had moved into the area. They were not attached to any of the family lines in the area who could have made their way easier. The man and woman were very quiet and kept to themselves. No one knew why they had moved there and since the couple did not offer any information, rumors were flying.

Tracilla was, as always, the leader in casting speculations. One day the woman was at the river washing clothes when Tracilla and her group passed by. Spying the woman, they went to the river pretending to cool their feet in the water.

As usual Tracilla was the first one to speak, "Good day, my friend, I hope you don't mind our cooling our feet so close to your wash area?"

The woman replied, "No, you are not in the way." The woman continued on with her work as if Tracilla or the other women did not exist.

Tracilla tried again to strike up a conversation, "My name is Tracilla, I am the wife of the High Priest Micah."

The woman only nodded and continued on with her work. Tracilla began to be annoyed, as she was not use to being ignored.

"Can we help you in any way? We know you are strangers to our land. If you need food, clothes or help with your children, it would be an honor for me to give." Tracilla inquired.

The woman seemed to blanch at the statement. Without a single word in reply, the woman arose and looked vacantly across the river. Then, as if being snatched back into this world unwillingly, the woman took her unfinished wash and climbed the hill on the short trek back to her home without a word.

Tracilla began to rant, "Did you see that? I extend my hand in friendship and help. What did she do? She turned and walked away from me without a word. From Me! Do you hear? From Me!"

Tracilla was enraged. This woman had the audacity to turn her back on her. A slap in the face of Tracilla would have been easier for her to bear than the obvious disregard of her self importance. In her mind, this woman should be groveling at her feet. The women around her did not know what to say. Some were secretly enjoying the rejection of Tracilla while others openly agreed with Tracilla to protect themselves from a similar attack to themselves.

"How dare she treat me like that! Is she stupid? Doesn't she know who she is talking to?" Tracilla was so furious she was spitting saliva from the sides of her mouth. She didn't realize how ridiculous she looked and her "friends" dare not tell her.

Thankful her rage was directed at someone else, Patisha said, "Tracilla, I can not believe someone could be that backward. You can look at your countenance and know you are someone of great stature and importance. She was outright dismissive of you. You should have told her about the sin she was committing." But in the back rooms of Patisha's mind she was laughing and dancing at the scene which had unfolded before her. In this most private of areas, the true person is always revealed.

Tracilla looked at the transparent woman and thought what a fool she is. Tracilla composed herself realizing she must not lose these "friends" by erratic behavior and exposing of her inner rage at being dismissed. She quickly grabbed the makeshift mantel of religious forgiveness and tolerance before she spoke. "Yes, you are right, Patisha. But I did not want to show unkindness to an obvious simpleton. Did you see the robe she had on? Obviously she is a woman of low means and from her manner low intellect also. Micah tells me they have no children. (Then why did she ask about caring for the children?, was in the minds of the women around her, but they dare not speak it.) Jehovah probably did not bless them because he knew they were not worthy."

While Tracilla was talking, everyone began putting on their most pious look and nodding their heads in agreement. Many of the women were just glad Tracilla had found a new target for her vindictiveness and it was not them. As long as they could keep the heat off of themselves, these women would gladly sacrifice anyone or anything. They dare not admit this to anyone for they knew they would take the chance of discovery. They kept these thoughts hidden in their minds and hearts, thinking no one would ever know. Little did they know their secret thoughts would be uncovered in the near future.

Tracilla continued with her attack of the woman for the next few weeks. Smiling and feigning graciousness to her face and stabbing her in the back at other times. She added untrue words to every encounter she had with the woman and even invented events which had never happened. Even if someone was with her, she knew her cronies would dare not challenge her. People began to stay away from the couple. They would whisper and laugh when they saw them. Some of the more vicious would make comments out loud when they passed. The couple did not respond as they were unaware the remarks were aimed at them.

This couple were grieving so much they could not see the snowball of animosity which was mounting toward them. I wonder if the people's consciences would have been seared if they had known the couple had recently lost all six of their beloved children. Would the people have been kinder if they had known the woman had held each child in her arms trying to stave away the fever which consumed it? Would the women have finally had the courage or character to stand up to Tracilla if they had known the heartache which enveloped this woman, causing her to care nothing for idle talk, food, or dress? Would the men have finally taken control of their wives if they had known this man had given up all to move to another province to remove his beloved grieving wife from the memories? Why must we know what drives a person's actions to show a simple kindness? Should our reactions be controlled from the inside out or from the outside in?

We will never know because the woman, overcome with sadness and despair, waded out into the river and drowned. Was this a purposeful act or did she go to retrieve a piece of clothing she lost while washing in the moving water? Only Yahweh knows. The man left the next week without a word, he was grieving so deeply. The people's tongues continued to wag for a few weeks until something more tantalizing came along. It was about this time that Jesus returned from the wilderness and began his ministry.

CHAPTER 3

When the man Jesus began his ministry he had been through and conquered most of the trials and tribulations the human race would ever face. He not only overcame, but became a stronger person because of them. He went through this so he could empathize with each individual and show them how to become conquerors in life. Would people have changed if they had known what had already been done for them? Maybe, but it wasn't to be because this man had even a bigger task to do for the unsuspecting people of the world. He would truly become the man of sorrows and this was done willingly for the world. I often wonder if some of his greatest sorrow came from being able to look into the hearts and minds of people. How he must have ached as he looked upon the blackness people hid inside. If I had been there and he looked in my heart, would he have smiled or cried? I'll never know and if I did know, the despair I would feel could possibly crush my soul.

Jesus went to live in Capernaum to fulfill the prophecy of Isaiah: Land of Zebulan and Land of Naphtah, the way to the sea, along the Jordan, Galilee of the Gentiles – the people living in darkness having seen a great light: on those living in the land of the shadow of death a light has dawned.

From that time on, Jesus began to preach, "Repent, for the kingdom of heaven is near."

Tracilla was in the marketplace when she learned of the young man's return. The marketplace was essential for the growing rawness inside of her. She would dip into the money coffers at home, without her husband's knowledge, and go off to buy some nonessential item she felt she must have. She would finagle and bargain with the merchants with a sharpness that took them by surprise. Many would give her what she wanted at base prices just to rid their stall of her viperous presence.

"Tracilla, have you heard of the return of Jesus? The one who was baptized by John over a month ago and then became missing? He is back and has become some type of roaming prophet. He is telling everyone they must repent and turn away from their sins. He keeps saying the kingdom of heaven is near." The lady watched intently to see Tracilla's reaction.

Tracilla stopped for a moment from inspecting a piece of fruit from a vendor's stall. She knew she must not show shock or displeasure in front of this woman. Even though most people had figured out Tracilla's nature long ago, people still pretended she was who she thought she was. They put on their religious mask and conversed with her just to try and get a reaction from her. Some even took delight in hearing her self aggrandizing drivel thinking they were so above her spiritually. When they were on the same level as her because they entangled themselves purposely in interactions with Tracilla yet feared to confront her.

"Oh, really, how wonderful he has been found. I know his mother is breathing a sigh of relief. What kind of son would do that to his mother? We must watch this young man to see that his actions match up to his message. Have a good day." Tracilla resumed the charade of gathering food for her family, but inside her mind was traveling a thousand miles a minute. For some reason this particular person was causing a tremendous urgency in her to quell his message to the people. The darkness was almost screaming inside of her head, "Stop Him! Stop Him!"

She hadn't thought much about this Jesus because she had been busy recently trying to destroy the business of a new peddler in town. Not knowing who he was dealing with, he had refused to come down on the price of a very expensive material Tracilla wanted to make a new robe from.

All of the old vendors knew Tracilla and what her evil tongue could do to their business, so they would always charge whatever price she wanted to pay. They would then make up the loss by charging the next customer extra. The new peddler was a man of principle and this practice would never have crossed his mind. The other peddlers had been growing tired of his honesty and fairness. They decided not to warn him of Tracilla and the damage she could cause. They felt this would straighten him out and get him in line with their practices.

Tracilla haggled with the new peddler for a week until he suggested she consider a different type of cloth that would be more in line with her finances.

"My dear lady, I have many types of cloth here. I am sure we can find something that would match your desire and your ability to pay." The merchant said from a place of concern to satisfy her desires and not to bring a hardship to her family. This suggestion went right to the core of Tracilla's greedy soul.

"What did you say? Do you know who you are talking to? Do you know how I can make you or break you? Are you that ignorant or just plain stupid? Do you know who my husband is? " Tracilla screamed at the merchant. The merchant became alarmed as Tracilla's rant morphed into a guttural mixture of unknown sounds. This made the hair on the back of his neck stand up and he began praying to Yahweh in his own mind to save him from woman.

Tracilla had always bragged to people about how much money she had and how much she spent on every article of clothing she had. (She did not tell how she blackmailed the merchants into giving her lower prices and even free items at times.) She would do anything to show the appearance of wealth. Now this impudent man was suggesting she buy a cheaper material. The man's integrity had just sealed his fate. Tracilla gathered her belongings after her outburst and without another word left the marketplace to plan her revenge.

Many of the women of the region had new clothes made from the cloth of the new peddler. They were all very happy with their new garments because everything the man had told them was true concerning their purchases. He was gaining a reputation as a man of honor. Even though his prices were higher, the quality of the material could not be matched. The women had been wondering why Tracilla had not obtained some of the wonderful merchandise. Little did they know Tracilla was spending the family into poverty. Her husband worked day and night to provide for his family while Tracilla was constantly spending the money trying to impress and intimidate anyone she could. Money had become her God and the need for more and more multiplied every day.

Fuming over the peddler's suggestion to her and driven by a force which was unstoppable, Tracilla went to the bank of the Sea of Galilee and scooped some of the sand from the shore into a container filled with certain herbs and oils. She mixed the concoction together until it was well blended. She spread it upon a large leaf and left it to dry in the sun. She then went to Patisha's house for the midday meal and silently cringed every time one of the ladies spoke of their purchases from the new vendor.

One of the bolder members of the group finally asked Tracilla why she had not been to see the new merchant. Two ladies smiled serenely as the question was asked because they had seen Tracilla twice arguing with the man over the price of the cloth. Secretly they knew Tracilla probably could not afford the material, but that was a thought that would never be heard aloud. Better a lowly peddler than them was in the back of their minds.

Tracilla braced herself when the question was put to her. She knew she had to answer without any hint of anger. "Oh, Micah has told me to refrain from buying any of the cloth because he has heard a few things about the man which causes him to worry. Some of Micah's very close and reliable business acquaintances have warned him about the man. They have not told Micah exactly what is wrong with the man or his merchandise, but they eluded to his making false claims about the purity of the cloth. I must submit to my husband's authority. It is only right in the eyes of the Lord." And with this Tracilla humbly bowed her head as if to punctuate the fact, "I am holy and you are not!" And for the first time Tracilla heard the darkness soothingly saying in her head, "Well done, my child."

The women began to look worried and glanced at their clothes with great suspicion. Inwardly Tracilla was thrilled that she had gotten the attention of the women. With a masterful, phony look of concern and bolstered by the darkness inside her, Tracilla continued, "Now don't worry about what I have said. I am sure it is just a silly misunderstanding. You know how competitive men of business are. They can't stand for anyone to outdo them. When men get together sometimes they say things off the top of their heads. If I hear of anything further I will be sure to let you know". If only Tracilla had known the women were not fooled by her statement, but Tracilla's husband's reputation was impeccable. A man of integrity and generosity. Using his name had put the doubt in their head. Surely Tracilla would not misrepresent this fine man. Tracilla's acceptance had always been precipitated by her husband's stellar character and now kept in place by the fear of Tracilla's tongue. Micah's marriage to Tracilla had allotted her many reprieves on her bad and vicious behavior.

The women left the house with a little less pride in their appearance. They were beginning to wonder what was wrong with their beautiful clothes. The colors did not seem as vibrant now and the feel was not as luxurious. The women had been duped by the treacherous words of one they should have already learned from. Had they not been around Tracilla long enough to know the falsehoods that spewed from her lips? Or maybe they chose to ignore the warning bells going off in their heads because of the many times Tracilla had tickled their ears with the latest gossip.

All they could do now was wait for more news from Tracilla and they certainly would not go back to the peddler for any more cloth. Another person's reputation sullied because of the silliness of man. Didn't the Lord warn people of the cruelty and harm of careless words?

News spread quickly the next day about the faulty fabric and there were many speculations about what was wrong with it. While the poison spread through the marketplace, Tracilla went to the river bank to retrieve her secret mixture. It had dried to a slick and grainy consistency. Tracilla hid it in the folds of her gown and happily went to make surprise visits on her friends.

As she went to each house, she laughed aloud at the mischief she was about to cause. Her conscience, long dead, did not bother her for one moment. Each friend greeted her with a kiss and welcomed her into their homes. She immediately told them Micah had discovered the truth about the peddler. The material was of such low grade, after a few days spots and stains would appear in the cloth when you wore it in the sun. The women hurriedly gathered their new clothes. Of course, Tracilla helped them, all the while touching the clothes with the hands she had rubbed liberally with her mixture.

After this, each woman and Tracilla took the clothes outside into the brightness of the day. There were spots and streaks all through the cloth causing the women to cry out in frustration or exclaim in anger. Tracilla made many visits that day and the next with the same thing happening over and over. Tracilla could hardly contain her excitement over how well her deception was working. Why some of the women were seeing spots and streaks in pieces of cloth Tracilla had not even touched! Tracilla was certainly a master of deceit!

After Tracilla had completed her mission, she proceeded to the marketplace and found an inconspicuous spot in full view of the new peddler. For a week, Tracilla spent her days watching the pitiful peddler return money to the irate women. As he looked at the cloth with spots and streaks, he could not imagine what could have caused such a thing. He returned money to everyone who brought their clothes in. He was an honest man. It never crossed his mind to refuse to return the money.

By the end of the week, he had no money and no merchandise,

for to resale the material was completely unthinkable to the man. He was completely ruined. He decided to leave town, not because of the loss of money, but because of the loss of his honor. Everyone called him a thief, a deceiver, a man with no soul. These were things he could not bear. He had spent his life building a reputation as an honest man of integrity. It was wiped away within days by lies. Lies spread from mouth to mouth, heart to heart.

As he packed his few belongings, the other peddlers watched and shivered at the realization of the true evil in the heart of Tracilla. They all breathed a sigh of relief that her wrath was not directed at them.

At the end of the week, Tracilla walked home by the river Jordan. She took the long way because she wanted to be alone to enjoy the thoughts of how powerful she was becoming. Her silly and careless remarks had grown into evil deeds and actions which could destroy anyone in her path. She felt invincible. She was laughing aloud when she heard John talking to a group of people.

Tracilla was so close to the truth and yet so far. If she had only listened to the young man walking through the region preaching repentance for the Kingdom of God is at hand, maybe her family would have been spared the heartache to come. How many times we miss the truth because we are so caught up in our righteous destruction of another human being. Tracilla would soon regret her ignoring of one of the greatest phenomenons of the world.

CHAPTER 4

John became bolder with his preaching which aggravated King Herod. John spoke the truth against King Herod with a forcefulness which the king could not abide. He denounced the King for taking his brother's wife. He spoke against the King in his sin. King Herod had overlooked the radical young man until now, thinking he was just odd and eccentric. When he began to speak of the King's personal sin, Herod became increasingly uncomfortable. He felt that John's preaching was acceptable for the common masses, but he should stay away from the speaking against royalty. Surely he knew that all of this nonsense of repentance was only for simple and ignorant people. They were the ones whose lives were so mundane and boring, they needed to believe in something other than their daily existence.

Herod's wife begged him to do something about the strange man and his preaching. Herod's wife was the reason he was in the position he had. Her family ties had been the catalyst. He knew he must listen to her or reap the consequences not only from her but her family also. Since Herod was king, he simply had him arrested. He thought this would pacify his wife and keep her from nagging him any longer. He never dreamed this woman would eventually be the impetus for him committing an even greater sin, which he would be tricked into doing because of his own weak will.

After John's arrest, Jesus went to Galilee to preach God's Good News. *"At last the time has come!"* he announced, *"God's Kingdom is near! Turn from your sins and act on this glorious news!"* The people were amazed at the authority with which this young man spoke. Many people were drawn to him and his words. His very presence seemed to electrify the area. People flocked to hear the words of the simple man of Galilee.

One day as Jesus was walking along the shores of the Sea of Galilee, he saw Simon and his brother Andrew fishing with nets, for they were commercial fishermen. Jesus called out to them, "Come, follow me! And I will make you fishermen for the souls of men!" At once, they left their nets and went along with him.

Simon and Andrew did not question the command or even say good bye to their families. They simply left their boats and followed the stranger. Something inside their heart told them that this was their destiny and this meeting had been planned from the beginning of time. As they walked with the man, they felt the most joy and peace they had ever experienced. Their minds and hearts began to drain of any earthly desire. Without words or actions, their fates were being sealed at that moment. I wonder if I would have followed so willingly or would I have asked for references and background information. Only God knows what I would have done and if he let me know, the sorrow would probably overcome me.

Walking a little farther up the beach, Jesus saw Zebedee's sons, James and John, in a boat. They were mending their nets. He called them too, and immediately the men left not only their boat but their father to join him. James and John also felt the same urgency in their souls to join this man in his journeys. Never in their lives had they been impulsive in their actions. This was so against their character, no one in their family would argue that the meeting was not of a divine nature.

Jesus and his companions traveled on to the town of Capernaum. On Saturday morning they went into the Jewish place of worship, the synagogue where he preached. The crowd of worshipers were not use to this type of preaching coming from anyone. He spoke as one of authority and did not back up his points with quotes from other speakers or writers. The people were amazed at what they were hearing.

One man who was possessed by a demon became very upset with the preaching and began shouting. The crowd was amazed as this man was a usually quiet man who put on an air of piousness, but as the words came forth from the Master's lips he had become increasingly troubled. An unknown voice came from the man's lips shouting in a most guttural sound. "Why are you bothering us, Jesus of Nazareth, have you come to destroy us demons? I know who you are – the holy Son of God!"

The people were horrified as they had not known this man was possessed. He had put on such an air of holiness in every service. They had known that his business dealings were of a questionable nature and that he was very cruel and heartless with his family. They had heard strange sounds coming from his fields at times, but had dismissed it as the wind or wild animals.

As the man continued his ranting and raving, Jesus curtly commanded the demon to say no more and to come out of the man. At that, the evil spirit screamed and convulsed the man violently and left him. He arose from the floor as if in a stupor. He looked around with a look of amazement to find himself the center of attention. He could not remember anything that had happened, but he did recognize the debt he owed the young unknown preacher. He was experiencing a freedom of spirit which he had not had in a long time. His wife ran to hug her husband as if he had been away for some time on a long journey.

Amazement and awe gripped the audience and they began discussing what they had just witnessed. "What sort of new religion is this?" they asked excitedly, "Why even evil spirits obey his orders!" The news of what he had done spread quickly through the entire area of Galilee.

The news hit Tracilla at a time when she was looking for more mischief to get into. She was becoming bored with her husband even though he did everything in his power to please her. Her children had become a chore which she dismissed to her handmaidens, sometimes not even speaking to them for days. Sometimes they would enter a room and Tracilla would not even acknowledge their presence because she was so absorbed with her own evil thoughts. Her whole life revolved around her needs and wants which were becoming increasingly insatiable. The more she received, the more she wanted and the more evil she committed, the more evil she became. She seemed to be existing on a never ending cycle of hurt, pain, pleasure which was never satisfied no matter how hard she tried to fill the ever widening hole in her soul. Now the darkness was enveloping her, feeding her ego and conscience with words that tickled her ears and made her feel more superior, more connected to a greater power which seemed to adore her.

When the news of the demon possessed man reached her, she was more than willing to listen. Only by the time it had reached her, the story had become somewhat distorted. It didn't really matter because Tracilla would change it anyway to meet her own devious agenda.

The next day Tracilla was to meet in the home of Kasha, wife of Mark, a physician of the tribe of Judah. Kasha was a beautiful woman known for her kindness and compassion. She was always trying to find the best in everyone and people were drawn to her because of this. Tracilla wanted to win this woman's favor because she also was effected by the purity of Kasha's spirit. Poor Kasha did not realize, in her naivety, she was inviting a poisonous snake into her home. Eventually even Kasha's sweet and innocent soul would be tarnished by the blackness of Tracilla's heart. I wonder if she had known, would she have withdrawn the invitation or in her mind feel she could help such a wayward person?

Tracilla was dressed in her finest and presenting a very pious face, when Kasha opened her door that morning. Kasha welcomed her with the graciousness she was known for. Tracilla was greeted warmly by the other women and Patisha made sure she was sitting in a place close by Tracilla.

Quickly the women began talking about the miracle which had happened in the synagogue in Capernaum. Each related their own version of the story which they swore was from the most reliable sources. If an outsider had been listening in, they would have been amused at the many different interpretations which were being told and how when each story was given, the women did not even question the illogical variances of the same tale. They very simply believed each detail, never questioning the truthfulness or plausibility of them.

Tracilla listened serenely, nodding knowingly with each story. She never commented or added any details as she wanted her version of the story to be told at a time when she was the complete center of attention. She wanted the women to hear and absorb every morsel of gossip (oops, information) she gave them. Tracilla had long ago realized that timing and presentation were key ingredients in spreading maliciousness. She had practiced her evil talent long enough to know that she could overpower even the most forceful of speakers if she timed it just right.

Tracilla was getting ready to enter the conversation and was waiting for one of the ladies to finish her version of the story. This woman was angering Tracilla because she was becoming extremely excited that the young preacher man could possibly be the true son of God. The King of Jews they had been waiting for. She was telling the women they must open their hearts and minds to the possibility because they did not want to miss such a great awaited revelation. The women were warming to the woman's open and honest appraisal of the possibility of the truthfulness of the man because of the miracle. Tracilla felt her time had come to put a stop to all of this speculation. She would not be uncovered as a liar because some silly woman wanted to fall for such foolishness.

With the sweetest of smiles, Tracilla interrupted the woman, "I am sure that in your heart you have the purest of intentions, but we must not mislead people about a matter of such importance. We have been waiting for a long time for the promised Messiah. We know he will be a King of our people so we must use our common sense. A King will be of noble birth. His birth will be rejoiced by all of heaven and earth. How can this young man be our promised Messiah when he was completely unknown until this time? His birth was a lowly one. I believe he was born in a stable because they did not have the money for an Inn. His father was well known in the region as an honorable man but not of royal blood. His mother is a sweet woman, but she has toiled all her life in a common way. Can you possibly believe Jehovah would send his son through such a line of lowliness? I think not. When the King comes we will all know it and be assured his arrival will not be announced in such an unruly way."

The women listened to Tracilla and the lightness of their hearts suddenly became heavy with the realization that Tracilla is probably right. They were being silly to become so overjoyed about such news. Tracilla, secretly, was amazed at how easy these women could be swayed with the slightest bit of wind. She decided she could tell these women anything and they would listen. They were so attuned to listening for the worst, believing the unbelievable and pouncing on the misfortune of another. Their lives had become the dumping ground for any piece of garbage which would take their minds off the emptiness in their hearts. I wonder if I would have stood up to Tracilla that day or have joined the women in losing their hope so easily. I really don't think I want to know.

Tracilla tilted her head and seemed to have a pained expression on her face as she continued, "You all know me, I am not one to dash anyone's hopes, but I have it on a reliable source that what happened at the synagogue was a hoax. It was planned by the man with his new found friends. You know the type of people he has associated himself with. These men are everyday fishermen. They are of common birth and not educated. They have latched themselves onto this man because of the emptiness of their lives. I am so glad my life is so full of happiness and love with my beloved husband and children so I don't search for such devilish antics to join in. They say the man was paid a sizable sum of money to play the part of one gripped by a demon. My sources tell me, he is a very dramatic type of fellow who often would disrupt the services with emotional pleas and theatrics. The whole thing was planned out and rehearsed in one of the fishermen's homes the previous night. They became so rowdy when they were together that night, many neighbors looked in out of concern for the safety of the family. They overheard and saw the exact same scene which was witnessed the next day in the synagogue. Now would a true King have to do that!"

As Tracilla weaved her tale, the disheartened women gradually warmed to hearing the filth which was spewing from her. By the end of Tracilla's story, the women were nodding their heads in disgust and horror about someone being so deceptive. They told Tracilla they were so glad she was able to find out the truth so they would not continue to believe such fallacy. Tracilla was now the star of the gathering as she had intended to be all along. To Tracilla it mattered not how she got this position, only that she had it and kept it. The darkness seemed very pleased with Tracilla's performance. Wait, did she actually feel that! A hand caressing her cheek to show love.

Kasha had been very quiet during the entire discourse. She had not offered any details or comments as the women spent the morning talking. The women never noticed this as they were so caught up in their usual game of pretend and destroy. They did not notice Kasha had lost her usual sweet smile as she listened to the cackling women. Kasha had become increasingly sorrowful as she realized her pleasant gathering had turned into a pit of venomous destruction. She knew her husband would be displeased as he did not speak unkindly or unjustly of anyone at any time. Her husband was a strong believer in surrounding yourself with people of likemindedness and he would not be happy about his precious Kasha being in the midst of such women.

There was something else Kasha had become increasingly uneasy about. She had not told the women about two of the fishermen being her own sweet cousins, Simon and Andrew. She had grown up with them and knew they were not the type of men these women were disparaging. She knew them as honest, hardworking and always seeking for the truth. She also knew the family had recently been thrown into turmoil because of their leaving with the man from Galilee. Simon had even left his wife of many years. His wife was trying to understand because she also knew Simon would have only done this for the most important reason. How could Kasha explain to these women when she couldn't understand why herself? She decided to keep quiet and continue her association with these women so she could possibly learn more of how this man could effect people so. Was this Kasha's reason or was she becoming entangled in the web of lies and deceit? Only Kasha and Jehovah know.

CHAPTER 5

Kasha did not know that Simon's wife had found peace in her husband's decision. It happened shortly after the miracle in the synagogue. *After leaving the synagogue, Jesus and his disciples went over to Simon and Andrew's home, where they found Simon's mother-in-law sick in bed with a high fever. They immediately told Jesus about her. Jesus went to her bedside and with a touch of his hand, the fever left her instantly. Jesus helped her to sit up. She was able to get up and prepare dinner for them.*

Simon's wife was overjoyed at the recovery of her precious mother. In her heart she finally relented and accepted the decision her husband had made. She knew it must be of the Most High God. Sometimes the Lord can teach great lessons through sickness and sorrow. Through the sickness of a loved one, Simon's wife learned of the compassion and love of our precious Savior. Her eyes were not blinded by the jealousy of separation in a relationship. She caught a glimpse of the whole scenario our Lord was putting in place at the moment of her mother's recovery. So many times we miss a lesson or a peek into the future because we are so caught up in our own selfish needs and desires.

News traveled quickly throughout the region of the miracles this man had brought about and by sunset the courtyard was filled with the sick and demon-possessed. People wanting to be healed, set free, or just witness the wonders surrounding this man. People walked for miles to reach this destination, drawn by an invisible cord connected to their innermost need. Among the crowd was a young couple by the name of Farah and Philibus. They were in Capernaum on business and had heard about the miracle at the synagogue. On the way home, they had seen the crowds traveling swiftly down a side street. Farah, being of a very curious nature, insisted they follow the people to see what was happening. They followed the crowd to a particularly lowly home on the outskirts of Capernaum. Philibus was ready to go home, as he knew they had a long journey, but Farah demanded they wait and see what all the commotion was about. As usual Farah got her way as she was very adept at manipulating her husband. Philibus just sighed and resigned himself to a long wait until his wife's curiosity had been satisfied. He had long ago learned it was better to go along with her escapades than to try and exert his authority over the home. Farah had been known to create very unpleasant scenes when she did not get her way.

Jesus looked out the window and saw the crowds. His heart was full of compassion and pain for the people and their sick loved ones. Jesus came out of the house and began to heal great numbers that evening. Many people were released from diseases and illnesses they had been plagued with for many years. There were children in the crowd who had never walked a day in their lives. Jesus touched their limbs and they began to run and jump with the joy only children can experience. Jesus opened the eyes of children who had never seen the blue of the sky or the green of the grass. When their eyes first beheld the glorious colors of the world, they screamed and wiggled with wonder. This brought a smile to Jesus because he knew how much his father must be enjoying the squeals of the children.

There were many people in the crowd possessed by demons. Jesus ordered the demons to come out of their victims. As he was commanding the demons to come out, he refused to allow them to speak. He knew these unearthly creatures recognized who he was. Just like the man in the synagogue, people were thrown into mighty convulsions when the demons left their bodies.

Farah and Philibus watched in amazement as the miraculous

occurrences happened all around them. Farah felt a desire to reach out to the Savior for healing of her viperous tongue, but then she withdrew when she realized she would have to give up control of her and her family's life. If there was anything in her life she would not do and that was to give up control. As the simple man of Galilee walked closer to her, she immediately turned to Philibus and told him they must go and she meant now. She began a fast walk back down the street with Philibus tagging along behind like a whipped dog.

Sometimes there are things in our lives stronger than our desire to discover spiritual truths. Would the bonds that held Farah have been weakened if Philibus had shown the strength of character needed for the head of the household? If Philibus had seen the road of destruction his wife was taking, would he have loved her enough to risk her wrath to save her? I wonder if Philibus would have walked back down the road, dragging Farah if he had an inkling of what was to be? Maybe he would have and maybe he wouldn't have. The miracles were freely given, yet pride can stand in the way of simply asking.

CHAPTER 6

The next morning Jesus was up long before daybreak and went out alone into the wilderness to pray. Later, Simon and the others went out to find him, and told him, "Everyone is asking for you." But he replied, "We must go on to other towns as well, and give my message to them too, for that is why I came."

So he traveled throughout the province of Galilee, preaching in the synagogues and releasing many from the power of demons.

Once a leper came and knelt in front of him and begged to be healed. "If you want to, you can make me well again," he pled. And Jesus, moved with pity, touched him and said, "I want to! Be healed!" Immediately the leprosy was gone — the man was healed!

Jesus then told him sternly, "Go and be examined immediately by the Jewish priest. Don't stop to speak to anyone along the way. Take along the offering prescribed by Moses for a leper who is healed, so that everyone will have proof that you are well again."

But as the man went on his way he began to shout the good news that he was healed; as a result, such throngs soon surrounded Jesus that he couldn't publicly enter a city anywhere, but had to stay out in the barren wastelands. And people from everywhere came to him there.

Sometimes in our exuberance to tell of a miracle we do not heed to obedience. So ingrained in our nature to talk incessantly, we can even ignore direct commands from the Holy One. We oftentimes justify it by saying we must share the good news so others will come to Christ. But as we see from the leper's story, he never took into account what his talking would do to the very one who had healed him. Jesus became a man with no home and no hope for the peace of being alone to meditate and collect his thoughts. He had to remain in barren wastelands with no comfort because this man did not listen to the Master's command. Maybe the Savior's ministry would have been a little easier if people had heeded his authority and obeyed.

People even ventured into the wastelands to see and be near the young man. Their thoughts were not on the fact that he would need rest and nourishment just as all humans, their focus was on their own selfish wants, needs, and curiosity. When they grew tired or needed food they just returned to their homes. Did they bring food to the master? Did they allow him to rest peacefully without being disturbed? When they saw him falter with weakness, did they show concern or only wait until he regained his strength to ask for more miracles? Did they offer to wash his clothes or bring him new ones? Did they offer him cool water to drink and soak his tired feet in? When they saw his needs, did they meet them as he met theirs or did they ignore the obvious signs of distress the human body can show?

As Jesus was ministering to the people in the desert, Tracilla was hearing the news of all the miracles performed by him. She was becoming more distressed as she knew her tiny secure world of control and manipulation was being threatened. Even though she had heard some bad reports about the incidents (most rumors she had personally started), she knew this man was not going to go away without extreme force. Her mind began to churn with plans to involve more important and powerful people.

The darkness was filling Tracilla's heart with thoughts of power. It was convincing her she was on a very important mission, to not destroy the religion she had comfortably acclimated to, but to protect the time honored laws and regulations which would usher in the God of her fathers. It had convinced her she was fighting for her lineage and she was the perfect one to stop this "heresy" brought into the nation by this man and his trickery. How many times we are fooled even when we are in the midst of the church? Could this happen to me or you? Is this what happens when we take our eyes off of God and put our focus on ourselves, our needs, our wants, and man made rules and regulations?

CHAPTER 7

That night, at mealtime, Tracilla began her assault on Jesus with her husband Micah. Micah was tired from working hard all day to provide for his family. Each day he found his money coffers becoming smaller and smaller. Each day he put forth twice the effort as the day before to restore the wealth he once had. He could not understand why the Lord would do this to him. He felt he was a just man who took care of his family and abided by the laws of the land. He had no one to talk this dilemma over with because he felt he would be condemned or chided for committing some sin in his life. So he kept everything hidden inside himself hoping he would be able to work harder the next day to bring back the blessing of the Lord to his household. Micah did not realize that his problem was sitting across the table from him. He did not know that Tracilla visited the money coffers to extract what she felt was her just due. Her plan was to blame the handmaiden if there was any question. She knew she could convince her husband of this. To her it would be a minor indiscretion to ruin the reputation of such a lowly person. Her needs or the life of someone beneath her? Surely anyone knew the answer to that in her own mind.

Tracilla could see that her husband was troubled with something but she was so intent on beginning her evil scheme of destruction she totally dismissed the worried look on her husband's face and began her spiel, "Micah, I know that you are preoccupied with matters of utmost importance but could I please trouble you with a small concern of mine?" Tracilla oozed with sweetness.

Micah was taken back, as his wife had not addressed him with such congeniality in a long time. She instantly won his attention as Micah was a person of strong commitment. He was committed to Tracilla and the children. Micah loved Tracilla with all of his heart. He remembered how she was when he first married her and had watched as she had changed through the years. He was blind to her faults because of this love or maybe he was scared of her like everyone else. Only Micah would be able to look inside his heart and tell the truth about that.

"Tracilla, you can always talk to me about anything. Anything that bothers you also bothers me as we are joined together as husband and wife," Micah replied.

Tracilla smirked inside herself and with her sweetest smile touched the arm of her husband. "I know you have heard about the young man who is going around the country claiming to be the Son of God. At first it seemed to be a very amusing pastime for the people, but it seems to be effecting our children. This concerns me greatly as I don't want the children's minds to be filled with heresy. It is hard enough raising children and protecting their minds without some person traveling the land with such preaching and tricks to fool people. Our children have been listening to other children whose parents are not as diligent as we are. These children have been taken to some of his so called sermons. The parents were absolutely fooled by what they saw and heard, so their children have followed their lead. Now our children want to go and see him. I just can't have this. I feel it would be blasphemy against our Holy God. I know, in all of your wisdom, you will know what I must do to protect our children."

Micah put on a look of concern and pretended to be giving the matter a lot of deep thought. After a few minutes of what he felt was adequate contemplation, he spoke, "This does seem to be a grave matter and I am so glad you have brought it to my attention. We absolutely do not want the minds of our children poisoned in any way against Jehovah. I will discuss the matter tomorrow with one of the teachers of law and ask his advice on how to handle the matter. I am sure they have heard about the man and are aware of the situation. You can rest assured we will take care of this."

Tracilla gave a humble nod of submission and thanked her husband for his kindness in listening to her. Micah's ego began to rise when he saw what his reply had done to his wife. Micah's plan was to dismiss this conversation but when he saw the loving expression on his wife, he decided he would really go to the teachers of the law the next day. In his mind, he felt this would keep his wife busy long enough so he could recoup some of his losses before she found out. Could deception and manipulation have entered into the innermost regions of Micah? Just as the serpent entered through the woman Eve and corrupted Adam.

Micah sat back with a satisfied grin on his face for he felt he had finally outwitted his wife. Little did he know that he himself had been outwitted. Soon Micah would regret the night he did not stand up to his wife and assert his authority. He would regret not having recognized the weakness in his wife and as a man listened and loved her while beseeching the Father to heal these weaknesses. Could Tracilla's innermost needs have been met if her husband had really looked at her and loved her unconditionally according to God's mandates and not man made ones?

The next day Micah learned that Jesus had returned to Capernaum. He heard that he was being besieged by crowds who wanted to hear his sermons and see his miracles. He went to the teachers of the law who agreed with Micah that a problem did seem to be arising because of this man called Jesus. They agreed to go with Micah to hear the young man and to personally appraise the situation.

Micah hurried home to tell Tracilla he would be going that very night with the teachers to hear Jesus. He assured her they would stop this man before he hurt anyone with his ridiculous claims. Tracilla ran from the room with her face covered. Micah thought she must be so overcome with emotion because of what he was doing. I wonder what Micah would have done if he had known she ran from the room because she could not constrain herself from laughing over how easily men can be manipulated.

CHAPTER 8

When Jesus returned to Capernaum and the people heard of this, he was bombarded with crowds at all times of the day. So many gathered there was no room left, not even outside the door, and he preached the word to them.

Some men came, bringing to him a paralytic, carried by four of them. Since they could not get him to Jesus because of the crowd, they made an opening in the roof above Jesus and after digging through it, lowered the mat the paralyzed man was lying on.

When Jesus saw their faith, he said to the paralytic, "Son, your sins are forgiven." Jesus knew that there were many people in the crowd who had come to defame and destroy him. He knew who they were and even what they were thinking. He also knew that Micah was in the crowd and his heart was saddened for the man. Jesus knew the part Micah would unknowingly take in bringing about what would eventually happen to him. Jesus was saddened because he knew that Micah was a pawn used by the ultimate evil one. I wonder if Micah would have left if he had known Jesus had already been pleading for him with the father. Would Micah have tried to change his wayward wife if he had known Jesus had already forgiven him for his part in the Savior's destruction?

Now some of the teachers of the law were sitting there, saying aloud inside of their heads, "Why does this fellow talk like that? He's blaspheming! Who can forgive sins but God alone!"

Immediately Jesus knew in his spirit this was what they were thinking in their hearts, and he said to them, "Why are you thinking these things? Which is easier, to say to the paralytic 'Your sins are forgiven,' or to say, 'Get up, take your mat and walk?' But that you may know that the Son of Man has authority on earth to forgive sins.....He said to the paralytic, "I tell you, get up, take your mat and go home." He got up, took his mat and walked out in full view of them all. This amazed everyone and they praised God, saying, "We have never seen anything like this!"

The teachers of the law were very chagrined at what Jesus had said to them. They were so absorbed in the attack on their importance, they had not even noticed Jesus had read their very thoughts. Micah had been very surprised at what he felt was an attack on the elders. He was only privy to one side of the conversation as he did not know what evil lay in the hearts of the teachers of law. Micah's reaction might have been very different if he could have been able to roam the darkness of the teachers' minds as Jesus could.

Jesus suddenly became lost in the crowd. No one could find him even though they looked earnestly. Jesus had become weary in mind and body. He had slipped off to be alone for awhile to recoup his strength. We often forget Jesus was God in a human body. The human body can just take so much stress, sleeplessness, hunger, and thirst until it has to be replenished and restored.

Once again Jesus went out beside the lake. Water seemed to calm his spirit and revive his soul. *A large crowd came to him and he began to teach them. As he walked along, he saw Levis, son of Alphaeus, sitting at the tax collector's booth. "Follow me," Jesus told him,* and once again another person followed the master without questioning.

While Jesus was having dinner at Levi's house, many tax collectors and "sinners" were eating with him and his disciples, for there were many who followed him. When the teachers of the law, who were Pharisees, saw him eating with the "sinners" and tax collectors, they asked his disciples, "Why does he eat with tax collectors and sinners?"

On hearing this, Jesus said to them, "It is not the healthy who need a doctor, but the sick. I have not come to call the righteous, but sinners."

The Pharisees pondered greatly on what the Master had told

them, but their preconceived ideas of what the Messiah would be overcame their ability to see or understand what he was trying to tell them. Sometimes our puffed up ideas of our own self importance rob us of opportunities to learn great truths and ideas which could change our whole future. I wonder if the Pharisees would have been more prone to listen and understand if their robes had not been made of the finest cloth. Sometimes positions of authority are more of a liability than an asset.

So he came for the sinners. Who was that? The tax collectors, the drunkards, the wife beaters, the husband manipulators, the prostitutes, the braggarts, the thieves, the murderers, the gossipers, or could he have also come for the Religious Hierarchy? Did they need saving also?

CHAPTER 9

Many days later, Micah heard of Jesus' scandalous association with sinners and tax collectors. It would be relayed to him by one of the Pharisees who had been present. This man conveniently would add his own twists and turns to the tale and distort what the man of Galilee had said. Micah would believe every word because he had unquestionable faith in the leaders of the Jewish Hierarchy. This unquenchable lust of the human race to destroy and mutilate another person with the tongue astounds the greatest minds, yet we feel we have done no harm because we have not touched their physical body. How many great and loving people have been deterred from their purpose in life because of this? How many people have given up and joined the herd because of this? How many nations have been destroyed because of this? On Judgment Day, will this be our greatest sin?

Micah's life was forever changed after the night he witnessed Jesus and heard his teachings. His conscience had been pricked, yet he had also seen what he believed an attack on the leadership. Having been raised to never question any type of authority he was deeply troubled because there was something inside of him which yearned to believe the Man of Sorrows. His upbringing and the fear of upsetting his wife would prove to be his undoing. No matter how much he wanted to follow Jesus and learn more, he did not have the strength to fight the powers which surrounded and controlled him.

Tracilla hung on every word her husband said about what

happened the night he went to Capernaum. As she was listening she was rearranging and reinventing every morsel of information Micah was giving her. She could tell her husband was troubled, yet she would not stop her questioning until her insatiable need was filled. She played the loving and concerned wife so she could influence her husband to become more involved in putting Jesus in his place. She stressed to Micah the importance of his role in accomplishing this. She played upon his ego by subtly hinting he may be the chosen one of Jehovah to prevent the heresy which Jesus was committing. Tracilla was so caught up in her tirade against the young preacher something very strange began to happen. Tracilla began to believe her own lies and theories. She truly began to believe she and her husband were on a mission from God to save the world from the unholy one himself. When her husband spoke, the words seem to turn and fly in the air until they changed and fit her own hellish plan of destruction. When Tracilla went to meet her friends the next day she did not have to lie anymore about Christ to reach her ultimate goal. Tracilla had truly crossed the line of reality because now even she believed her own lies.

Micah watched in amazement as his wife began to babble incoherently and then compose herself. Every time he spoke she would try to repeat what he said. The only problem was it was not what he was trying to tell her. The more he tried to make her understand what he was saying the more adamant she was she had heard him correctly. Their conversation ran on through the night with Micah trying to make her understand and Tracilla trying to convince him she had heard correctly. By the night's end, Micah was not even sure of what had occurred in Capernaum. Many of the things Tracilla said seeped into his mind and planted themselves forever to be there. The next day when he met with the Pharisees who had seen Jesus at the late supper, he was more susceptible to the overblown story of Jesus and his rowdiness. Do we set our own family up sometime to being susceptible to outside influences by weakening their minds with malicious drivel? Should we not strengthen their minds and wills with truths that will keep their feet upon the rock? If he looked into my home, would he be pleased or saddened?

We protect our homes, our families, our possessions, but do we protect the most precious thing God has given us, our minds. The Lord tells us to fill them with good things, precious things, things of good report. Do we truly do this when we listen to the idle conversation of others?

CHAPTER 10

Now John's disciples and the Pharisees were fasting. Some people came and asked Jesus, "How is it that John's disciples and the disciples of the Pharisees are fasting, but yours are not?"

Jesus answered, "How can the guests of the bridegroom fast while he is with them? They cannot, so long as they have him with them. But the time will come when the bridegroom will be taken from them, and on that day they will fast.

No one sews a patch of unshrunk cloth on an old garment. If he does, the new piece will pull away from the old, making the tear worse. And no one pours new wine into old wineskins. If he does, the wine will burst the skins, and both the wine and the wineskins will be ruined. No, he pours new wine into new wineskins."

One Sabbath Jesus was going through the grainfields, and as his disciples walked along, they began to pick some heads of grain. The Pharisees said to him, "Look, why are they doing what is unlawful on the Sabbath?"

He answered, "Have you never read what David did when he and his companions were hungry and in need? In the days of Abiathar the high priest, he entered the house of God, and ate the consecrated bread, which is lawful only for priests to eat. And he also gave some to his companions."

Then he said to them, "The Sabbath was made for man, not man for the Sabbath. So the Son of Man is Lord even of the Sabbath."

The young man of Galilee confused the Pharisees by speaking

in parables. This angered them because they prided themselves for their intellect and wisdom. How dare this foolish man babble on about things only they understood. If the masses began to follow this unruly man, there would be riots and revolts against time honored laws. In their small minds they could not understand that Christ had come to fulfill the law, not do away with it. If they had only laid down their self pride they could have seen that the law pointed to him. How many times we miss the prize because our eyes are on the breaking of rules and regulations, many of which are put in place by man himself. We put ourselves in our own prisons and castigate the one who is holding the key to open the door. We become our own jailers, spitting at and rebuking the ones who have chosen to walk free in the light.

CHAPTER 11

Tracilla had become a prisoner of her own lies and innuendo. People who claimed to love her only turned their heads. When they saw her coming they did not have the strength of will to leave or even try and dispute the things which she was saying. So in their weakness their own minds became infiltrated with the filth of her tongue. So many times we feel if we just stand and remain quiet we are ok. That is one of the most dangerous sins. It is the sin of omission which is a sin which puts you directly under the authority of God. You can't explain it away, you can't blame it on any one else, and you can't run from it. God loves you enough to not allow this.

Tracilla appointed herself the guardian of truth and began to follow Jesus wherever he went. With the reluctant blessing of her husband she left with fellow conspirators many times a week to meet and make plans for the destruction of Jesus or to follow him and listen to his sermons always finding some type of quote to distort and reconstruct to her own devilish plans. Farah and Patisha followed Tracilla as much as they could. Philibus would often escort the women on their escapades as he knew it would not look right for the women to be seen out alone after dark. In the beginning Micah would go along with Tracilla, but soon grew weary of hearing such evil things about a man he had a secret yearning to follow. Philibus became the unofficial male guardian of the women as Farah would make his life miserable if he did not comply.

The Pharisees listened to the women whenever they requested a hearing. They were secretly pleased with the gathering storm which the women were creating. It made their work much easier and later on they could blame it on the cacklings of stupid women if anything went wrong. Both groups were using each other to reach their mutual goal of destroying Jesus.

One time Jesus went into the synagogue, and a man with a shriveled hand was there. Tracilla's group and the Pharisees were there looking for a reason to accuse Jesus, so they watched him closely to see if he would heal him on the Sabbath.

Jesus said to the man with the shriveled hand, "Stand up in front of everyone." Then Jesus asked them, "Which is lawful on the Sabbath: to do good or to do evil, to save life or to kill?" But they remained silent. The question had caught them off guard as they thought they were hidden in the crowd. When Jesus spoke he looked straight into their eyes and they squirmed as he looked into the dark recesses of their minds.

He looked around at them in anger and, deeply distressed at their stubborn hearts, said to the man, "Stretch out your hand." He stretched it out and his hand was completely restored. Then the Pharisees went out and began to plot with the Herodians how they might kill Jesus.

When the Pharisees mentioned the word kill, Tracilla had a faint nudge at her conscience. She had never really considered how this could lead to the physical death of a person. She had never been involved in any physical harm of a person, or so she thought. She had always felt she was alright in her quests because she only ruined people emotionally, financially and spiritually. After their run ins with her they could always get up and walk away, hoping to start over elsewhere. This time she would help in the actual physical death of a person. Even though her conscience was pricked momentarily, she quickly brushed it aside, believing it must be done to protect the Law of Jehovah. In her convoluted mindset, this was a justifiable cause of the planned murder.

CHAPTER 12

Jesus withdrew with his disciples to the lake, and a large crowd from Galilee followed. When they heard all he was doing, many people came to him from Judea, Jerusalem, Idumea, and the regions across the Jordan and around Tyre and Sidon. Because of the crowd he told his disciples to have a small boat ready for him, to keep the people from crowding him. For he had healed many, so that those with diseases were pushing forward to touch him. Whenever the evil spirits saw him, they fell down before him and cried out, "You are the Son of God!" But he gave them strict orders not to tell who he was.

Tracilla ran from the meeting when she heard this. There was something inside of her screaming the same phrase. She fought with herself not to scream the words aloud as other people were doing before her. To prevent this she feigned sickness and ran to the back of the crowd. She felt weak but as soon as she left the presence of Christ her strength began to return. She could even feel a new surge of energy which sustained her on her walk home. She decided her mind was playing tricks on her and she must guard it against the heresy which she was encountering. Besides she felt she had enough ammunition to begin a new reign of hate and spitefulness.

When she reached home Tracilla was not alarmed to see a small crowd at her home. Her thoughts had assured her she was the leader of a Holy Mission so there were certain inconveniences which would go along with it. Even though she had walked a long way and was tired, the opportunity to fill fresh ears with her important information only she could give refreshed her.

Tracilla dusted off her robe, put on her most pious look, and entered the room. The greeting she received was not what she expected. The looks were ones of pity and sorrow. Instantly Tracilla could sense these people were not there for the delicious morsels of gossip she had to give them. There was something terribly wrong.

"Why are you here so late? What is wrong? I can tell by your looks something has happened! Tell me! Tell me now!" Tracilla demanded.

The people turned away as she spoke as they did not want to be the one to break the news. Tracilla looked from person to person. She then realized these people were her neighbors. People she had shunned before. None of her close friends or family members were there. This eased her mind as she felt if there was something disastrous surely her close friends and family would be there. It never entered her mind that she had estranged herself from every member of her family over the years because of supposed slights or cruelties she had heaped upon them. Her close friends were out doing what they thought was the will of the Lord. They were at different group meetings spreading the lies of heresy committed supposedly by the Man from Galilee.

As Tracilla turned to go to the next room Micah entered with a look of sorrow she had never seen before. This struck at her heart for she knew only something happening to her or the children would bring such a look of woe upon him.

"Micah, what has happened? No one will tell me! Tell me now! What has befallen you?" Tracilla screamed.

Micah took a deep breath which he hoped would hold back the tears. As he spoke there was a tremor in his voice as if he were trying not to cry or lash out in rage. "Tracilla, it is Ashon, she has fallen ill. The doctors do not know what is wrong with her. They are trying to help her but feel we must be prepared for the worse."

Tracilla felt as if someone had hit her hard in the chest. She could not speak, she could not breathe, she could not even scream. When she regained her composure she ran to her daughter's room to find the doctors leaning over her shaking their heads.

Tracilla demanded they do something. She screamed at them to save her child but as she was raving at the doctors Ashon slipped into the next world soundlessly. Tracilla became like a madwoman. She screamed and cursed at the doctors. She railed at Micah for not protecting her child. She tore her clothes in agony. She got in the bed with Ashon begging her to breathe. She rocked her back and forth hoping the warmth of her body would return life to her child. When people tried to take Ashon from her she fought them with the strength of ten men.

"Leave this room. You are disturbing her. She only needs to sleep. When she wakes up she will be all better. I know this! I know this! I KNOW THIS! The Lord would not do this to me. I am doing his will. He has only put her to sleep for a while. You doctors do not know anything. I do. A mother knows! A mother knows! Go! Leave us alone! She needs her mother! SHE NEEDS HER MOTHER!" Tracilla screamed between begging Ashon to awake.

Tracilla's last statement would ring in her ears for the rest of her life. She needs her mother! She needs her mother! Ashon did need her mother. Two days before she had come to Tracilla to show her a bite on her leg. She tried to describe the spider which had bitten her but Tracilla was getting ready to go out that afternoon with her friends to gather more about Jesus. She half listened to Ashon and never did look at the place on her leg. She told Ashon not to be a baby. It was just a little bite. She told her to wash it and she would see about it later. When she came home Tracilla was told by her handmaiden that Ashon had gone to bed early. She never questioned this as she was very tired from all of the exchanges which had gone on throughout the day. She was secretly relieved she did not have to be bothered by the child. The next day she left early as she had lots of important meetings and gatherings to go to. She did not even look into Ashon's room. She had happily gone off to do her evil deeds.

Micah would never know of this for Tracilla would banish this handmaiden, laying the blame of Ashon's death on her. Micah, in his sorrow, never questioned the fact Tracilla had not known her child was sick for two days. When people came to the handmaiden's defense and told Micah how she had sat with the child the whole time, he could not hear through the fog of loss he felt in his soul. All around people knew the real person responsible for Ashon's death was Tracilla, yet they were powerless to do anything to help the poor handmaiden as she was thrown to the wolves. She was found guilty of murder and stoned in the streets while Tracilla wore her mourning garments with her head held high.

After the shock of Ashon's death dulled, Tracilla began to wonder how such a thing could have happened to her. In her warped thinking, she reasoned Jesus must have done this because he knew she was against him. He must have used some type of evil witchcraft to bring about the death of her child. She became convinced of this and used it as fuel in her quest against him.

If Tracilla could have looked into the Savior's mind she would have cried out with the agony of a thousand mothers. The Savior had been waiting for her to bring the child to him. He had planned to save the child so Tracilla would not have to go through the torture she was in. His heart ached for her even with all the evil she had done against him. If Jesus had healed Ashon, would Tracilla have changed her heart or would she have used it against him? We will never know as Tracilla had not even known of Ashon's illness because she was gone from home.

While Tracilla and Micah were burying and mourning their child, many things were happening in the region.

CHAPTER 13

Mark 3:13-34 King James Version (KJV)

13 And he goeth up into a mountain, and calleth unto him whom he would: and they came unto him.

14 And he ordained twelve, that they should be with him, and that he might send them forth to preach,

15 And to have power to heal sicknesses, and to cast out devils:

16 And Simon he surnamed Peter;

17 And James the son of Zebedee, and John the brother of James; and he surnamed them Boanerges, which is, The sons of thunder:

18 And Andrew, and Philip, and Bartholomew, and Matthew, and Thomas, and James the son of Alphaeus, and Thaddaeus, and Simon the Canaanite,

19 And Judas Iscariot, which also betrayed him: and they went into an house.

20 And the multitude cometh together again, so that they could not so much as eat bread.

21 And when his friends heard of it, they went out to lay hold on him: for they said, He is beside himself.

22 And the scribes which came down from Jerusalem said, He hath Beelzebub, and by the prince of the devils casteth he out devils.

23 And he called them unto him, and said unto them in parables, How can Satan cast out Satan?

24 And if a kingdom be divided against itself, that kingdom cannot stand.

25 And if a house be divided against itself, that house cannot stand.

26 And if Satan rise up against himself, and be divided, he cannot stand, but hath an end.

27 No man can enter into a strong man's house, and spoil his goods, except he will first bind the strong man; and then he will spoil his house.

28 Verily I say unto you, All sins shall be forgiven unto the sons of men, and blasphemies wherewith soever they shall blaspheme:

29 But he that shall blaspheme against the Holy Ghost hath never forgiveness, but is in danger of eternal damnation.

30 Because they said, He hath an unclean spirit.

31 There came then his brethren and his mother, and, standing without, sent unto him, calling him.

32 And the multitude sat about him, and they said unto him, Behold, thy mother and thy brethren without seek for thee.

33 And he answered them, saying, Who is my mother, or my brethren?

34 And he looked round about on them which sat about him, and said, Behold my mother and my brethren!

35 For whosoever shall do the will of God, the same is my brother, and my sister, and mother.

Mark 4 King James Version (KJV)

4 And he began again to teach by the sea side: and there was gathered unto him a great multitude, so that he entered into a ship, and sat in the sea; and the whole multitude was by the sea on the land.

2 And he taught them many things by parables, and said unto them in his doctrine,

3 Hearken; Behold, there went out a sower to sow:

4 And it came to pass, as he sowed, some fell by the way side, and the fowls of the air came and devoured it up.

5 And some fell on stony ground, where it had not much earth; and immediately it sprang up, because it had no depth of earth:

6 But when the sun was up, it was scorched; and because it had no root, it withered away.

7 And some fell among thorns, and the thorns grew up, and choked it, and it yielded no fruit.

8 And other fell on good ground, and did yield fruit that sprang up and increased; and brought forth, some thirty, and some sixty, and some an hundred.

9 And he said unto them, He that hath ears to hear, let him hear.

10 And when he was alone, they that were about him with the twelve asked of him the parable.

11 And he said unto them, Unto you it is given to know the mystery of the kingdom of God: but unto them that are without, all these things are done in parables:

12 That seeing they may see, and not perceive; and hearing they may hear, and not understand; lest at any time they should be converted, and their sins should be forgiven them.

13 And he said unto them, Know ye not this parable? and how then will ye know all parables?

14 The sower soweth the word.

15 And these are they by the way side, where the word is sown; but when they have heard, Satan cometh immediately, and taketh away the word that was sown in their hearts.

16 And these are they likewise which are sown on stony ground; who, when they have heard the word, immediately receive it with gladness;

17 And have no root in themselves, and so endure but for a time: afterward, when affliction or persecution ariseth for the word's sake, immediately they are offended.

18 And these are they which are sown among thorns; such as hear the word,

19 And the cares of this world, and the deceitfulness of riches, and the lusts of other things entering in, choke the word, and it becometh unfruitful.

20 And these are they which are sown on good ground; such as hear the word, and receive it, and bring forth fruit, some thirtyfold, some sixty, and some an hundred.

21 And he said unto them, Is a candle brought to be put under a bushel, or under a bed? and not to be set on a candlestick?

22 For there is nothing hid, which shall not be manifested; neither was any thing kept secret, but that it should come abroad.

23 If any man have ears to hear, let him hear.

24 And he said unto them, Take heed what ye hear: with what measure ye mete, it shall be measured to you: and unto you that hear shall more be given.

25 For he that hath, to him shall be given: and he that hath not, from him shall be taken even that which he hath.

26 And he said, So is the kingdom of God, as if a man should cast seed into the ground;

27 And should sleep, and rise night and day, and the seed should spring and grow up, he knoweth not how.

28 For the earth bringeth forth fruit of herself; first the blade, then the ear, after that the full corn in the ear.

29 But when the fruit is brought forth, immediately he putteth in the sickle, because the harvest is come.

30 And he said, Whereunto shall we liken the kingdom of God? or with what comparison shall we compare it?

31 It is like a grain of mustard seed, which, when it is sown in the earth, is less than all the seeds that be in the earth:

32 But when it is sown, it groweth up, and becometh greater than all herbs, and shooteth out great branches; so that the fowls of the air may lodge under the shadow of it.

33 And with many such parables spake he the word unto them, as they were able to hear it.

34 But without a parable spake he not unto them: and when they were alone, he expounded all things to his disciples.

35 And the same day, when the even was come, he saith unto them, Let us pass over unto the other side.

36 And when they had sent away the multitude, they took him even as he was in the ship. And there were also with him other little ships.

37 And there arose a great storm of wind, and the waves beat into the ship, so that it was now full.

38 And he was in the hinder part of the ship, asleep on a pillow: and they awake him, and say unto him, Master, carest thou not that we perish?

39 And he arose, and rebuked the wind, and said unto the sea, Peace, be still. And the wind ceased, and there was a great calm.

40 And he said unto them, Why are ye so fearful? how is it that ye have no faith?

41 And they feared exceedingly, and said one to another, What manner of man is this, that even the wind and the sea obey him?

CHAPTER 14

A short time after Ashon's burial Tracilla got up early to dress in her finest to meet Patisha, Farah and a reluctant Kasha at Farah's house. As she was dressing, Micah entered the room and asked his wife where she planned to go. Tracilla continued dressing as she answered Micah.

"Farah is having a small gathering at her home. I just felt it would help me to leave the house and my grief for a brief time. It will help me to be in the company of my friends." Tracilla said.

"Absolutely not! You will stay in this house for the customary period of mourning, Tracilla. Our daughter is dead but for a short while and you are going out among the public. We will not disgrace our daughter's memory by breaking the rules of official mourning. I will send a messenger to Farah's home to say you will not be there." Micah adamantly replied.

Tracilla stopped dressing and turned to face her husband. She had never been spoken to like this before. She was surprised to see a man with such a look of resolve on his face she knew she dare not defy. Micah seemed changed in some way. No longer did he look upon Tracilla with a look of affection. His very stature seemed to have been strengthened by the loss of his daughter. Grief mixed with strength. What an odd combination but a combination of emotions which was almost palpable.

She decided to play upon his position of authority and manipulate him through his ego. "Of course, my husband, you are correct. I don't know what I was thinking. I have been under such sorrow I can not even think straight. You are right, we must not besmirch the memory of our precious daughter. I will begin my life again when it is proper and holy in the eyes of God. I know you are the one who is thinking straight. Please forgive me, my love." Tracilla meekly replied.

A look of shock came upon Tracilla's face when Micah said, "Tracilla, don't try to play your games with me. My daughter is dead. This shroud of sorrow is making me see things in a much different light. She might not be dead if you had been at home to see about her. I will not lose any more because of your need to spread evil. I will stay with you because divorce is such a shame upon the family name, but things will change or I will put you out in the street."

Tracilla could not move or speak as she listened to her husband's anger spew out at her. She had always been able to get her way with Micah. He had never come against her in such a way. She decided this is just because of their deep loss. She would pretend to humbly submit for a period of time and things would return back to normal. Micah turned with a look of disgust as Tracilla lowered her head in supposed submission.

Micah had finally risen up and asserted his God given authority over his wife. It took a tragedy to do this. Things might have been different if he had done it earlier in their marriage. Later events could possibly have been avoided if he had not been so weak in his leadership in the home. But if things had been different he probably would not have agreed to the union in the first place. When his family had started the talk of marriage with Tracilla, he might have run for the hills preferring to remain alone in solitude rather than be joined with her. Then the Lord would have had to choose another person to use in his great plan to cause the greatest event in the world. The Lord is even able to use evil to reach his own goals of good and unity. He is truly an awesome God.

With the loss of her daughter and the rejection of her husband, Tracilla should have started to reflect on her own misdeeds. Instead she began to rationalize in her mind how all of the misfortunes which had befallen her were the results of the man called Jesus. She decided she would take this time of mourning and devise even more evil rumors against Jesus. She would have to be even more crafty as Micah was now watching her. But Tracilla had begun to believe in her own sense of power and felt this would be a minor set back. Had the darkness completely overcome her? Was there any hope for her?

Micah sent a messenger to Farah's house to inform the women Tracilla would not be joining them. He did not give any excuse only that she would not be there. When the messenger returned, Tracilla sent him back with another message. One Micah would not know about as he was still in deep mourning. The message Tracilla sent would draw Patisha and Farah deeper into an alliance with her, while driving Kasha away.

Tracilla's message was short and to the point. "Come as soon as you can. Tell your husbands nothing, lie if you have to." Patisha's conscience was pricked a little by the message, yet it did not stop her from rushing to Tracilla's home. Farah was not bothered at all about deceiving her husband. It had become an ordinary occurrence for her, but Kasha was horrified at the very thought of lying to her husband. Their relationship was built on trust and honor. She immediately left Farah's home without even a good bye. Choices can change your future in a moment and long term consequences can be suffered for a simple, silent choice.

CHAPTER 15

As Tracilla sat at home devising schemes inside her head, Jesus was traveling the country performing miracles and loving people which would play right into Tracilla's hands. Would Jesus have stopped if he had known this or did he continue because he did know this? Remember he could see the whole picture while Tracilla only saw her blurred, distorted portion of it. His ultimate sacrifice becomes so much more precious because he knew and loved us enough to continue walking toward that fateful day.

Mark 5:1-20 King James Version (KJV)

5 And they came over unto the other side of the sea, into the country of the Gadarenes.

2 And when he was come out of the ship, immediately there met him out of the tombs a man with an unclean spirit,

3 Who had his dwelling among the tombs; and no man could bind him, no, not with chains:

4 Because that he had been often bound with fetters and chains, and the chains had been plucked asunder by him, and the fetters broken in pieces: neither could any man tame him.

5 And always, night and day, he was in the mountains, and in the tombs, crying, and cutting himself with stones.

6 But when he saw Jesus afar off, he ran and worshipped him,

7 And cried with a loud voice, and said, What have I to do with thee, Jesus, thou Son of the most high God? I adjure thee by God, that thou torment me not.

8 For he said unto him, Come out of the man, thou unclean spirit.

9 And he asked him, What is thy name? And he answered, saying, My name is Legion: for we are many.

10 And he besought him much that he would not send them away out of the country.

11 Now there was there nigh unto the mountains a great herd of swine feeding.

12 And all the devils besought him, saying, Send us into the swine, that we may enter into them.

13 And forthwith Jesus gave them leave. And the unclean spirits went out, and entered into the swine: and the herd ran violently down a steep place into the sea, (they were about two thousand;) and were choked in the sea.

14 And they that fed the swine fled, and told it in the city, and in the country. And they went out to see what it was that was done.

15 And they come to Jesus, and see him that was possessed with the devil, and had the legion, sitting, and clothed, and in his right mind: and they were afraid.

16 And they that saw it told them how it befell to him that was possessed with the devil, and also concerning the swine.

17 And they began to pray him to depart out of their coasts.

18 And when he was come into the ship, he that had been possessed with the devil prayed him that he might be with him.

19 Howbeit Jesus suffered him not, but saith unto him, Go home to thy friends, and tell them how great things the Lord hath done for thee, and hath had compassion on thee.

20 And he departed, and began to publish in Decapolis how great things Jesus had done for him: and all men did marvel.

There were great losses and gains that day. The owners of the livestock lost their worldly possessions, the possessed man lost his life of hopelessness and the onlookers lost their argument of spiritual ignorance. Some people walked away angry, others in awe, others became believers that day while others dismissed it as coincidence and one man walked away joyful. I wonder which group I would have been a part of if I had been there.

CHAPTER 16

For months Tracilla played the part of the dutiful wife. She was so convincing Micah began to let down his guard. Many people in the community were fooled by the now complacent Tracilla. They felt the death of her daughter must have reached the innermost parts of her soul and worked a miraculous transformation. Tracilla was surely a master of deception. Even her own household servants were taken back by the change. Only Patisha and Farah knew the true reason for the subservient attitude of Tracilla. Even they began to put on the facade of being the dutiful wife and mother. They were quite surprised at what they could finagle out of their husbands by doing this. The husbands must have talked among themselves because they began to pat each other on the back for the change in their homes. Little did they know they were being used by the very ones who claimed to love them so much.

Farah and Patish had the most freedom of movement and because of this Tracilla would use them as messengers for her. In her home she would devise new and evil rumors to spread throughout the land and Farah would keep her abreast of the latest comings and goings of the Messiah. The women were very good at balancing the two roles of gossip monger and loving wife. Patisha had the most trouble because she tended to run off at the mouth without thinking. Tracilla and Farah were constantly at her to hold her tongue until the appropriate time. This fault of Patisha's would be the reason the women's husbands would be present at what would happen in the future to them.

Tracilla had convinced herself Ashon's death was caused by the evil one to prevent her attack on his servant, Jesus. When Jesus banished the evil spirits into the herd of pigs, she used this as a way to strengthen her case against him. She spun a web of spiritual deception which fooled even the most learned of religious scholars. She took actual text of the Jewish law and twisted it to convince many that Jesus could not possibly be the one he claims. The law said he would come to lead his people out of spiritual darkness. Surely he would not bring such financial ruin to one of his own. Because most of the Jewish community in the last few years had been more concerned about gaining wealth and prestige rather than spiritual enlightenment, they were easily fooled with Tracilla's reasoning. They had left the spiritual side of their lives up to the ones they felt were the experts – Pharisees and Sadduccees. Jewish businessmen began to conspire with the teachers of the law to curtail the young preacher man in fear they would lose their own resources. Little did they understand the plans which were being laid by the inner core of the supposed religious group.

The teachers of the law were amazed at the convincing tales which Tracilla could tell. They almost believed themselves, even though they knew the truth. The lies and deceit were flying in the air and the wind of anarchy was infiltrating every walk of society. Tracilla was amazed at the power she had even when she was in forced confinement. She decided then and there the talents she possessed were surely worth money. She would demand this next time she met with the teachers of the law. Then she would not have to depend upon the whim of her now distant husband. She would have her own money source to draw upon so she could gain the independence she now craved.

Farah and Patisha continued to do her bidding while she was in confinement. They looked forward to the importance they felt when they were escorted into the chambers of the teachers of the law.

There was no waiting for them. Whenever they entered they were immediately led into a meeting with the teachers. Sometimes they even dared to change or add a little to the story given to them by Tracilla. They felt she would never know as when her confinement was up there would always be something new to tell. They did not feel they were lying, only using any means to a righteous end. God would surely overlook their minor indiscretion compared to what Jesus of Nazareth was doing. Farah and Patisha soon began to believe their own lies to assuage the guilt building inside of them. So many times we claim to know the mind of God to justify something we want to do.

CHAPTER 17

While Farah and Patisha were meeting with the synagogue rulers, they were unaware that one of the rulers was at that moment seeking the help of the very one they were conspiring to destroy. Jarius was going for the help of Jesus for his dying daughter. He was desperate to find someone to cure her. In desperation he sought to find out if the miracles he was hearing about were real or only tricks of the mind.

When Jesus had again crossed over by boat to the other side of the lake, a large crowd gathered around him while he was by the lake. Then one of the synagogue rulers, named Jarius, came there. Seeing Jesus, he fell at his feet and pleaded earnestly with him, "My little daughter is dying. Please come and put your hands on her so that she will be healed and live." So Jesus went with him.

He went in and said to them, "Why all this commotion and wailing?" The child is not dead but asleep." But they laughed at him.

After he put them all out, he took the child's father and mother and the disciples who were with him, and went in where the child was. He took her by the hand and said to her, "Talitha koum!" (which means, "Little girl, I say to you, get up!") Immediately the girl stood up and walked around (she was twelve years old). At this they were completely astonished.

He gave strict orders not to let anyone know about this, and told them to give her something to eat.

Jairus was overjoyed to see his precious child alive and well. He decided right then to put a stop to the plot against the man called Jesus. When Jesus gave strict orders not to let anyone know about this his heart sank. Surely this young man does not know about the evil being conspired against him. He could possibly die because of it. But Christ was firm in his orders not to tell and he felt he owed the man his unquestioning loyalty because of the miracle performed on his beloved daughter. He would not be able to tell about the miracle he had witnessed but that did not stop him from causing as much confusion as he could in their devilish plot.

A direct command from the very lips of the one he had been waiting for. A learned, humble man who knew where to go when his heart was breaking, yet he questioned the authority of this man after seeing a miracle before his very eyes. Devising ways to circumvent what had to happen. Sometimes we need to question less and obey more.

CHAPTER 18

After one whole year of being in confinement for mourning, Tracilla was chomping at the bits to leave the house. Micah had agreed it was time for her to enter the world and begin her normal routine. Little did he know what her normal routine consisted of. Micah had spent the year looking at himself and questioning what had caused the tragedy in his life. Tracilla had spent the year stewing in self pity, vengeance, and anger.

Tracilla immediately went to Farah's house and began to make plans about a secret meeting the next day with the synagogue rulers. Tracilla planned to speak before the group and implore them to end this young man's mass delusion. She planned not to hold back anything, for the year in seclusion had given her time to think about every word, every expression and every move she would make when she had the opportunity. Now her long awaited chance had come and she could hardly wait until the next day. She felt Farah and Patisha had done an adequate job in her absence, but now the real power would be unleashed.

Tracilla came home in plenty of time to take over the preparation of the evening meal. She did not want anything to arouse Micah's suspicion for the next day was too important to be hindered by her silly husband's obsession with home and family. Her handmaidens had spent most of the day preparing the evening meal, yet when Micah came home Tracilla took all of the credit, even berating the girls in front of Micah for their laziness. The girls just shook their heads realizing the change they had believed to have happened with Tracilla was just a facade. They went back to their quarters determined to keep their suspicions to themselves and just stay out of her line of fire when possible.

Tracilla was very preoccupied that night, thinking about the next day's meeting. Micah asked what was the matter and she told him the day's outing had tired her and reminded her of places she had been with Ashon. Micah accepted her phony excuse and tried to be understanding of his wife's feelings. In the year of seclusion, Micah had been totally fooled by the supposed change in Tracilla. This had lulled him into a sense of false security and he was even now falling back into the old habit of overlooking Tracilla's obvious lies. If he had been more observant, he would have realized that the meal before him would have taken all day to prepare and now Tracilla was saying she had been out the whole day.

That night Tracilla lay awake until the early morning hours rehearsing in her mind over and over what she would say the next day. She did not know that she had an enemy in the midst of the synagogue rulers. Someone who knew she was a liar and a cheat. Tracilla felt she had the support of all the teachers of the law. Tomorrow she would realize she must be more careful of where she put her trust.

Early in the morning Tracilla arose to begin the morning meal. She wanted Micah to awake to her cooking his meal. She wanted to make sure his mind was at ease and he was not suspicious. Today was too important to be confined to the house. Micah arose and found her in her everyday robe. This was the robe she wore when she planned to stay home and do extensive cleaning. Micah felt this was a good thing for her. It would keep her mind off of the absence of Ashon. Micah would have been surprised if he knew that Tracilla rarely thought of her daughter. The only time it entered her mind was in conjunction of how she could use the death to hurt Jesus.

After Micah had left for the day Tracilla hurried to her room to change her clothes. She wanted to wear her best mourning robe. She felt this would win the sympathy and compassion of the teachers. She instructed her servants on what to prepare for the evening meal. She planned to take credit for cooking it so they must prepare it just as she instructed them to. If Micah were to appear for any reason during the day, they were to say she went for a special ingredient for the meal. They must rush him along, by telling him this was a surprise meal for his love throughout the long year of mourning. Her handmaidens lowered their heads in obedience to her commands and also in grief for her open deception to her husband.

Having set everything into place, Tracilla covered her face and hurried to pick up Farah and Patisha. They walked the long way to the synagogue and avoided places in which they would be recognized. It would not do for anyone to report to their husbands about their rushing toward the synagogue. They had convinced their husbands they had laid down all plans to harm Jesus of Nazareth. Open lying surely would be overlooked when you are on a mission of such a holy nature.

They entered the synagogue by the back door while many miles away Jesus was traveling toward his hometown. I wonder if Jesus knew the time was drawing close and just wanted to visit the place where he grew up just one more time. Sometimes we like to travel back to a time and place where we had comfort and security. Sometimes it helps us in the road ahead.

CHAPTER 19

Mark 6:1-29 King James Version (KJV)

6 And he went out from thence, and came into his own country; and his disciples follow him.

2 And when the sabbath day was come, he began to teach in the synagogue: and many hearing him were astonished, saying, From whence hath this man these things? and what wisdom is this which is given unto him, that even such mighty works are wrought by his hands?

3 Is not this the carpenter, the son of Mary, the brother of James, and Joses, and of Juda, and Simon? and are not his sisters here with us? And they were offended at him.

4 But Jesus, said unto them, A prophet is not without honour, but in his own country, and among his own kin, and in his own house.

5 And he could there do no mighty work, save that he laid his hands upon a few sick folk, and healed them.

6 And he marvelled because of their unbelief. And he went round about the villages, teaching.

7 And he called unto him the twelve, and began to send them forth by two and two; and gave them power over unclean spirits;

8 And commanded them that they should take nothing for their journey, save a staff only; no scrip, no bread, no money in their purse:

9 But be shod with sandals; and not put on two coats.

10 And he said unto them, In what place soever ye enter into an house, there abide till ye depart from that place.

11 And whosoever shall not receive you, nor hear you, when ye depart thence, shake off the dust under your feet for a testimony against them. Verily I say unto you, It shall be more tolerable for Sodom and Gomorrha in the day of judgment, than for that city.

12 And they went out, and preached that men should repent.

13 And they cast out many devils, and anointed with oil many that were sick, and healed them.

14 And king Herod heard of him; (for his name was spread abroad:) and he said, That John the Baptist was risen from the dead, and therefore mighty works do shew forth themselves in him.

15 Others said, That it is Elias. And others said, That it is a prophet, or as one of the prophets.

16 But when Herod heard thereof, he said, It is John, whom I beheaded: he is risen from the dead.

17 For Herod himself had sent forth and laid hold upon John, and bound him in prison for Herodias' sake, his brother Philip's wife: for he had married her.

18 For John had said unto Herod, It is not lawful for thee to have thy brother's wife.

19 Therefore Herodias had a quarrel against him, and would have killed him; but she could not:

20 For Herod feared John, knowing that he was a just man and an holy, and observed him; and when he heard him, he did many things, and heard him gladly.

21 And when a convenient day was come, that Herod on his birthday made a supper to his lords, high captains, and chief estates of Galilee;

22 And when the daughter of the said Herodias came in, and danced, and pleased Herod and them that sat with him, the king said unto the damsel, Ask of me whatsoever thou wilt, and I will give it thee.

23 And he sware unto her, Whatsoever thou shalt ask of me, I will give it thee, unto the half of my kingdom.

24 And she went forth, and said unto her mother, What shall I ask? And she said, The head of John the Baptist.

25 And she came in straightway with haste unto the king, and asked, saying, I will that thou give me by and by in a charger the head of John the Baptist.

26 And the king was exceeding sorry; yet for his oath's sake, and for their sakes which sat with him, he would not reject her.

27 And immediately the king sent an executioner, and commanded his head to be brought: and he went and beheaded him in the prison,

28 And brought his head in a charger, and gave it to the damsel: and the damsel gave it to her mother.

29 And when his disciples heard of it, they came and took up his corpse, and laid it in a tomb.

The tongue is a powerful instrument. It can build up and it can tear down. John was using his words to bring the Jews to repentance, to prepare for the coming of Christ. He spoke the truth and it seared the conscience of Herodias until using her own daughter in a murder plot was perfectly acceptable. How we don't want to hear the truth but run toward rumor and innuendo at all costs. We fight to clear our conscience by committing the most atrocious acts and then wonder why we still feel guilty.

CHAPTER 20

Patisha and Farah bowed their heads submissively as they entered the room where the rulers were gathered around a long table, while Tracilla walked in with her head held high as if she owned the world and everything in it. As the women came into the room, all heads turned and all were pleased to see them but one.

The head of the council, Mosha, was the first to speak, "Good morning, dear ladies and what glad tidings do you have to give us today?"

"Good morrow, my lord, we are here with our ever growing concern of the man called Jesus. It is our understanding he is performing some remarkable feats of banishing demons. I have a personal account of this I would like to share," Tracilla boldly began.

"Our concern of the antics of this man is also growing daily. We know you are fine and reputable citizens who have helped us greatly in our pursuit of truth and justice," Mosha smiled as he spoke these words for he knew this would reach the ego of Tracilla and cause her to be even more vicious. He understood Tracilla completely and had been using her for his own personal reasons. Mosha planned to stop this young man and claim all the glory. His plan was to use and discard anyone he could to achieve his ultimate goal. Tracilla unknowingly played right into his hands.

Tracilla was flattered by the obvious high regard Mosha was displaying toward her. This gave her more confidence in what she was about to say.

"If I could have but a small portion of your time, I would like to share what I know personally of the deceptions of this so called Son of Man. As you all know I lost my precious daughter Ashon one year ago. At the time I had become concerned about many of the things I was hearing about Jesus. I was afraid of the heresy entering my home and into the minds of my own children. I began to go whenever I could to hear him teaching. I was appalled at many of the things I heard and could see through many of his so called miracles. I decided I could not stand by and allow such obvious tricks to be played upon my friends and family. I began meeting with certain groups of people to plan ways to protect ourselves. I regret to say I must have become too vocal because many strange and frightening things began to happen to me and my family."

"I was visited once by one of his followers and threatened. I was told if I didn't stay at home and keep my mouth shut, my family would fall into sorrow and ruin." Tracilla stopped here for a dramatic pause to accentuate the statement she had just made.

At this obvious lie, Patisha and Farah raised their heads and looked on in astonishment. They knew if this had really happened to Tracilla, she would have sung it from the rooftops. Patisha began to realize what a deceptive net was being woven by Tracilla. She began to feel very awkward and uncomfortable. She wanted to run and wash her hands of the dirty mess but her character was still too weak to make her legs turn and go. Farah, on the other hand, was even more energized by the outright lie. She felt this meant that all moral rules and laws were being thrown out the window. She almost smiled with glee at all the evil she realized she would be involved in. Both women stared at Tracilla with different emotions as she continued.

"Being the gentle woman that I am, I was shocked into silence. The visitor left immediately and no one had seen the strange man. I kept this close to my heart as I feared for the safety of my family. After days of meditation and prayer, I decided the Lord would protect me as I was doing nothing wrong. I did not tell my husband as he is so protective, he would have immediately confronted Jesus.

With all of his followers and the people being fooled by him I was afraid for my husband's very life."

"The next time Jesus was close by, I decided to go where he was teaching. I wanted him to see my presence and know I was not afraid of him. I listened to his foolishness but when he began his so called miracles I could not contain myself. I began talking to the people who were around me and telling how he accomplished his tricks. Jesus saw me speaking with the people and I guess he could tell by their faces he was losing their loyalty. Such a look of anger came across his face, I felt I was looking into the very face of Satan himself."

"I immediately left as I feared for my safety. As I was walking down the road to my home, I was surrounded by the most roguish group of men. They began to taunt me and poke at me. I did not reply and continued walking home. They followed me to the last turn to my home. It was such a relief to know I was so close to safety. They all turned to go back, but one of the men caught my arm and whispered into my ear, "I would watch my children closely, if I were you." Being a mother, I turned and slapped his face with all of my might. He merely laughed and turned to join the others. I turned and ran home. Needless to say I could not sleep that night for continually checking on my children."

All of the men at the table, but one, were transfixed by the story being told by Tracilla. She was so convincing in every detail. The men did not know they were being hypnotized by deception. As Tracilla spoke, Patisha began to pale and almost fainted. Farah was becoming so excited she had to hold her arms tight for she wanted to jump with glee.

Tracilla had never had such a prestigious group of listeners and for a year she had planned this tale. She had gone over each detail day after day. She could have recited it in her sleep, she knew it so well. She knew the next part was the one in which she must put on her best performance. It was crucial, this part must be told from the heart of a grieving mother.

"My children are my heart. But I love the Lord too. I am a righteous woman, who has kept all the laws faithfully all of my life. I never dreamed I would ever be put in such a position. I never dreamed I would bury one of my own children."

At this, Jarius could not contain himself any longer. Trying to hold back his anger, he sternly asked, "Are you implying Jesus had anything to do with the loss of your daughter?"

Tracilla was taken back by the way in which Jarius asked his question. She had expected great sympathy, but this man seemed to exude a hostility toward her. This was something she had not expected or planned for.

"My Lord, I am not making any accusations. I am just telling the facts the way they happened. I am depending on you in all your wisdom to make a judgment. These things happened a few days before my lovely daughter Ashon became ill. After she had died, we learned the servant who had been tending her was related to one of the followers of Jesus. We also learned the servant had given some type of concoction to my daughter the day she became ill. She said it was to counteract the poison from a spider bite. But, my lords, there was no mark upon my child's body. She had not been bitten by any spider. The handmaiden was executed for her crime but I don't believe she acted alone. I feel she was put up to do this awful crime by outside forces. I may be a mother in mourning who is not thinking straight, but for a whole year I have thought of nothing else. The only conclusion I can come to is Jesus was behind my child's death." Tracilla bowed her head in supposed grief. The men turned their heads from her sorrow.

Jarius was the only one who continued to look at Tracilla. He could not believe such a charge was being made against the very man who had saved his own daughter. Yet the master had told him to tell no one. But in his mind, he began to think of ways to discredit this hysterical woman.

CHAPTER 21

While Tracilla was ending her speech:

Mark 6:30-52 King James Version (KJV)

30 And the apostles gathered themselves together unto Jesus, and told him all things, both what they had done, and what they had taught.

31 And he said unto them, Come ye yourselves apart into a desert place, and rest a while: for there were many coming and going, and they had no leisure so much as to eat.

32 And they departed into a desert place by ship privately.

33 And the people saw them departing, and many knew him, and ran afoot thither out of all cities, and outwent them, and came together unto him.

34 And Jesus, when he came out, saw much people, and was moved with compassion toward them, because they were as sheep not having a shepherd: and he began to teach them many things.

35 And when the day was now far spent, his disciples came unto him, and said, This is a desert place, and now the time is far passed:

36 Send them away, that they may go into the country round about, and into the villages, and buy themselves bread: for they have nothing to eat.

37 He answered and said unto them, Give ye them to eat. And they say unto him, Shall we go and buy two hundred pennyworth of bread, and give them to eat?

38 He saith unto them, How many loaves have ye? go and see. And when they knew, they say, Five, and two fishes.

39 And he commanded them to make all sit down by companies upon the green grass.

40 And they sat down in ranks, by hundreds, and by fifties.

41 And when he had taken the five loaves and the two fishes, he looked up to heaven, and blessed, and brake the loaves, and gave them to his disciples to set before them; and the two fishes divided he among them all.

42 And they did all eat, and were filled.

43 And they took up twelve baskets full of the fragments, and of the fishes.

44 And they that did eat of the loaves were about five thousand men.

45 And straightway he constrained his disciples to get into the ship, and to go to the other side before unto Bethsaida, while he sent away the people.

46 And when he had sent them away, he departed into a mountain to pray.

47 And when even was come, the ship was in the midst of the sea, and he alone on the land.

48 And he saw them toiling in rowing; for the wind was contrary unto them: and about the fourth watch of the night he cometh unto them, walking upon the sea, and would have passed by them.

49 But when they saw him walking upon the sea, they supposed it had been a spirit, and cried out:

50 For they all saw him, and were troubled. And immediately he talked with them, and saith unto them, Be of good cheer: it is I; be not afraid.

51 And he went up unto them into the ship; and the wind ceased: and they were sore amazed in themselves beyond measure, and wondered.

52 For they considered not the miracle of the loaves: for their heart was hardened.

CHAPTER 22

It seemed the more miracles and good Jesus spread, the more the darkness in Tracilla grew. As Jesus was feeding the people with the five loaves of bread and two fish, Tracilla was sitting in her comfortable home with Patisha and Farah reviewing what had happened that morning. Tracilla had gone away from the meeting disturbed by the hostility of one of the religious rulers by the name of Jarius. She could not understand why this man, who did not know her, could treat her with such disdain. She quickly put this on the back burner of her mind and instead decided to concentrate on the pressing need of stopping Jesus.

Patisha was uncommonly quiet while Farah was energized to the point of frenzy. She could not stop talking and pacing the room. Since there were no boundaries of morality anymore, she was making up some of the most outlandish tales ever heard. She seemed to be bouncing them off of Patisha and Tracilla to see if she should tone them down a little so they would be believable. The more she talked, the more Patisha seemed to go inside of herself. Tracilla and Farah did not notice this as they were too involved in fabricating lies to spread throughout the region.

Tracilla had planned to ask for some type of monetary help at the end of the meeting, but with the opposition of Jarius, she decided she would put this off until later. She felt she had done enough that day to push the rulers into doing something to stop Jesus. The council had promised her they were looking into the matter and would let her know what their decision would be to punish Jesus and his followers for the death of her child.

As the day grew later, Tracilla had to ask Patisha and Farah to leave. She knew Micah would be returning home soon and he would not appreciate finding them there. Patisha was grateful she could finally escape the growing madness while Farah almost cried in dismay that their fun should have to be cut short. Tracilla assured Farah she would be in touch with her as soon as she heard from the council.

Micah came home to find Tracilla in the back room attending to his nightly meal. She had changed clothes and pretended she had spent all day preparing his favorite meal. The servants would not dare dispute this or they would have suffered from Tracilla's tongue the next day. Micah was pleased his wife was finding joy in her wifely duties and praised her throughout the meal. Tracilla accepted the compliments with not a tinge of conscience. It had died long ago.

Tracilla would not have been pleased if she had been able to hear what was being said in the council next week. Mosha and Jarius seemed to be at opposite ends of any discussion of the accusation brought by Tracilla. The rest of the council simply sat in silence listening to the two men argue day in and day out. Neither would give an inch and neither could persuade any member of the council to his side. Finally the men agreed they would continue to personally follow Jesus and see if there was any suspicious behavior. Mosha felt this would allow all members to see and hear first hand the tricks and heresy used by Jesus. Jarius, on the other hand, felt the members would see firsthand the innocence and great compassion of the teacher.

When Tracilla heard the council had not come to any formal plan of punishment for Jesus, she was livid. In her mind, she felt she had supplied them with enough evidence to put the man and his followers to death. How dare these men try to interfere with the will of God! When she reported their decision to Farah, even Tracilla was surprised at the anger displayed by her friend. She ranted and raved about the stupidity of men and how if anything was to be done women always had to do it. Patisha was secretly relieved that the council had used wisdom and not swallowed Tracilla's obvious lies. Patisha could sit back quietly and continue her participation in what she felt was the harmless gossip of women.

CHAPTER 23

Mark 7 King James Version (KJV)

7 Then came together unto him the Pharisees, and certain of the scribes, which came from Jerusalem.

2 And when they saw some of his disciples eat bread with defiled, that is to say, with unwashen, hands, they found fault.

3 For the Pharisees, and all the Jews, except they wash their hands oft, eat not, holding the tradition of the elders.

4 And when they come from the market, except they wash, they eat not. And many other things there be, which they have received to hold, as the washing of cups, and pots, brasen vessels, and of tables.

5 Then the Pharisees and scribes asked him, Why walk not thy disciples according to the tradition of the elders, but eat bread with unwashen hands?

6 He answered and said unto them, Well hath Esaias prophesied of you hypocrites, as it is written, This people honoureth me with their lips, but their heart is far from me.

7 Howbeit in vain do they worship me, teaching for doctrines the commandments of men.

8 For laying aside the commandment of God, ye hold the tradition of men, as the washing of pots and cups: and many other such like things ye do.

9 And he said unto them, Full well ye reject the commandment of God, that ye may keep your own tradition.

10 For Moses said, Honour thy father and thy mother; and, Whoso curseth father or mother, let him die the death:

11 But ye say, If a man shall say to his father or mother, It is Corban, that is to say, a gift, by whatsoever thou mightest be profited by me; he shall be free.

12 And ye suffer him no more to do ought for his father or his mother;

13 Making the word of God of none effect through your tradition, which ye have delivered: and many such like things do ye.

14 And when he had called all the people unto him, he said unto them, Hearken unto me every one of you, and understand:

15 There is nothing from without a man, that entering into him can defile him: but the things which come out of him, those are they that defile the man.

16 If any man have ears to hear, let him hear.

17 And when he was entered into the house from the people, his disciples asked him concerning the parable.

18 And he saith unto them, Are ye so without understanding also? Do ye not perceive, that whatsoever thing from without entereth into the man, it cannot defile him;

19 Because it entereth not into his heart, but into the belly, and goeth out into the draught, purging all meats?

20 And he said, That which cometh out of the man, that defileth the man.

21 For from within, out of the heart of men, proceed evil thoughts, adulteries, fornications, murders,

22 Thefts, covetousness, wickedness, deceit, lasciviousness, an evil eye, blasphemy, pride, foolishness:

23 All these evil things come from within, and defile the man.

24 And from thence he arose, and went into the borders of Tyre and Sidon, and entered into an house, and would have no man know it: but he could not be hid.

25 For a certain woman, whose young daughter had an unclean spirit, heard of him, and came and fell at his feet:

26 The woman was a Greek, a Syrophenician by nation; and she besought him that he would cast forth the devil out of her daughter.

27 But Jesus said unto her, Let the children first be filled: for it is not meet to take the children's bread, and to cast it unto the dogs.

28 And she answered and said unto him, Yes, Lord: yet the dogs under the table eat of the children's crumbs.

29 And he said unto her, For this saying go thy way; the devil is gone out of thy daughter.

30 And when she was come to her house, she found the devil gone out, and her daughter laid upon the bed.

31 And again, departing from the coasts of Tyre and Sidon, he came unto the sea of Galilee, through the midst of the coasts of Decapolis.

32 And they bring unto him one that was deaf, and had an impediment in his speech; and they beseech him to put his hand upon him.

33 And he took him aside from the multitude, and put his fingers into his ears, and he spit, and touched his tongue;

34 And looking up to heaven, he sighed, and saith unto him, Ephphatha, that is, Be opened.

35 And straightway his ears were opened, and the string of his tongue was loosed, and he spake plain.

36 And he charged them that they should tell no man: but the more he charged them, so much the more a great deal they published it;

37 And were beyond measure astonished, saying, He hath done all things well: he maketh both the deaf to hear, and the dumb to speak.

CHAPTER 24

The religious leaders met together after the encounter with Jesus to discuss what had been said to them. Many were outraged at the insolence of the young man. How dare he call them hypocrites when they had faithfully followed the Jewish law for so long. The man had not shown them any respect at all. In fact he had talked down to them as if they were the ones who should be judged.

Mosha was the first to speak, "I'm afraid, dear brothers, we have a serious problem in our midst. This young man is going to cause an insurrection among the people. We must put a stop to it. He is very disarming and persuasive. The people are being fooled by him because he is using his limited knowledge of the law and twisting it to please the masses. He speaks in parables which is further confusing the people. We, as leaders of the Jewish faith, must put an end to this. We do not want our people putting their faith in a false prophet."

The rest of the group nodded their heads, except for Jarius. Jarius had also been disturbed by what the master had said to them, but for a completely different reason. For many years he had felt the same thing in his heart, that they were following traditions passed down by man, while ignoring the true commands of a Holy God. Mosha took Jarius' silence as an agreement to what he had just said.

While Jarius was searching inside his heart for some type of reconciliation to what the master had said and how his own life was being lived, the Pharisees and religious leaders agreed they must bring this matter before the King. They felt Herod would surely be sympathetic to their plight because he had put to death the other insurrectionist, John the Baptist.

They also decided to pick people who had a talent of persuasion and pay them to go among the people and spread rumors about the young man and his followers. The first person to come to their mind was Tracilla and her friends as she had been doing this all along. They knew a person could be destroyed with just the right rumors spread in just the right way.

All but Jarius were in agreement they must continue to follow and observe Jesus in his ministry. To go before the king, they must have evidence to present to him. The more they had the more convinced the King would be to stop Jesus.

When Tracilla was called before the council the next day, she was thrilled to hear of their decision. She was also honored she was chosen to be in the center of the plot to discredit Christ and his followers. She was also glad they brought up the matter of payment and she would not have to mention it. With the council's mandate, she knew she would be able to get Micah's permission to help. He would not go against the Jewish authority. Tracilla was walking on clouds when she returned home that day. She felt the young man of Galilee's days were numbered and she wanted to be there when the final curtain came down.

She spent the rest of the week gathering people to help her and planning her strategies on how to best attack Jesus. Farah was just as happy as Tracilla to be involved with such an important task. Patisha was devastated when she heard. She had hoped the religious leaders would not involve them anymore if they decided to bring Jesus up on charges. When Tracilla told her what they had asked her to do, she almost fainted. Patisha knew she had gone as far as she was willing to go. She would now have to find the strength to make a stand against the one she feared the most. Patisha knew she would be ostracized for the rest of her life by Tracilla and anyone associated with her, but she also knew she could not be involved in such evil as they had planned for Jesus.

Tracilla took the news from Patisha with a great calm. She told Patisha she understood and would not hold it against her in any way. Patisha went away feeling she had done the right thing and God had been gracious in not allowing her to be the target of Tracilla's spite. In Patisha's simple mind she felt she would not suffer any consequences for the part she had played in hurting Jesus. Little did she know, she was going to be Tracilla's next project after she was finished destroying Jesus. But before this could happen, Patisha had to face the consequences of a just and loving God for her deeds against his very own son.

CHAPTER 25

Mark 8 King James Version (KJV)

8 In those days the multitude being very great, and having nothing to eat, Jesus called his disciples unto him, and saith unto them,

2 I have compassion on the multitude, because they have now been with me three days, and have nothing to eat:

3 And if I send them away fasting to their own houses, they will faint by the way: for divers of them came from far.

4 And his disciples answered him, From whence can a man satisfy these men with bread here in the wilderness?

5 And he asked them, How many loaves have ye? And they said, Seven.

6 And he commanded the people to sit down on the ground: and he took the seven loaves, and gave thanks, and brake, and gave to his disciples to set before them; and they did set them before the people.

7 And they had a few small fishes: and he blessed, and commanded to set them also before them.

8 So they did eat, and were filled: and they took up of the broken meat that was left seven baskets.

9 And they that had eaten were about four thousand: and he sent them away.

10 And straightway he entered into a ship with his disciples, and came into the parts of Dalmanutha.

11 And the Pharisees came forth, and began to question with him, seeking of him a sign from heaven, tempting him.

12 And he sighed deeply in his spirit, and saith, Why doth this generation seek after a sign? verily I say unto you, There shall no sign be given unto this generation.

13 And he left them, and entering into the ship again departed to the other side.

14 Now the disciples had forgotten to take bread, neither had they in the ship with them more than one loaf.

15 And he charged them, saying, Take heed, beware of the leaven of the Pharisees, and of the leaven of Herod.

16 And they reasoned among themselves, saying, It is because we have no bread.

17 And when Jesus knew it, he saith unto them, Why reason ye, because ye have no bread? perceive ye not yet, neither understand? have ye your heart yet hardened?

18 Having eyes, see ye not? and having ears, hear ye not? and do ye not remember?

19 When I brake the five loaves among five thousand, how many baskets full of fragments took ye up? They say unto him, Twelve.

20 And when the seven among four thousand, how many baskets full of fragments took ye up? And they said, Seven.

21 And he said unto them, How is it that ye do not understand?

22 And he cometh to Bethsaida; and they bring a blind man unto him, and besought him to touch him.

23 And he took the blind man by the hand, and led him out of the town; and when he had spit on his eyes, and put his hands upon him, he asked him if he saw ought.

24 And he looked up, and said, I see men as trees, walking.

25 After that he put his hands again upon his eyes, and made him look up: and he was restored, and saw every man clearly.

26 And he sent him away to his house, saying, Neither go into the town, nor tell it to any in the town.

27 And Jesus went out, and his disciples, into the towns of Caesarea Philippi: and by the way he asked his disciples, saying unto them, Whom do men say that I am?

28 And they answered, John the Baptist; but some say, Elias; and others, One of the prophets.

29 And he saith unto them, But whom say ye that I am? And Peter answereth and saith unto him, Thou art the Christ.

30 And he charged them that they should tell no man of him.

31 And he began to teach them, that the Son of man must suffer many things, and be rejected of the elders, and of the chief priests, and scribes, and be killed, and after three days rise again.

32 And he spake that saying openly. And Peter took him, and began to rebuke him.

33 But when he had turned about and looked on his disciples, he rebuked Peter, saying, Get thee behind me, Satan: for thou savourest not the things that be of God, but the things that be of men.

34 And when he had called the people unto him with his disciples also, he said unto them, Whosoever will come after me, let him deny himself, and take up his cross, and follow me.

35 For whosoever will save his life shall lose it; but whosoever shall lose his life for my sake and the gospel's, the same shall save it.

36 For what shall it profit a man, if he shall gain the whole world, and lose his own soul?

37 Or what shall a man give in exchange for his soul?

38 Whosoever therefore shall be ashamed of me and of my words in this adulterous and sinful generation; of him also shall the Son of man be ashamed, when he cometh in the glory of his Father with the holy angels.

Mark 9:1 King James Version (KJV)

9 And he said unto them, Verily I say unto you, That there be some of them that stand here, which shall not taste of death, till they have seen the kingdom of God come with power.

CHAPTER 26

When Micah was told by Tracilla about the council's decision, he reluctantly gave his permission. Tracilla knew she would have continued even Micah had not agreed, but she did not tell her husband this. She would let him believe it was his decision for as long as it helped her. Micah was becoming the least of her worries. Micah left the room with his shoulders downtrodden as if he wore the weight of the world on them. Little did he know, the control for the future of the world was being waged in his own household.

Tracilla sat up the rest of the night planning her attack. With the council behind her, she felt a sense of power that energized her. Thoughts invaded her mind throughout the night, unbelievable spoutings from unearthly forces. Tracilla welcomed them as she would a long lost love. She felt they were emanating from the genius of her very own mind. Little did she know that many of the thoughts and ideas she devised that night came from the very pit of hell. Would she have continued if she had known or run screaming from her house? Satan was very clever that night. He only showed himself cloaked in the evilness of Tracilla's own mind.

When the sun began to show itself over the peaks of the mountains outside the window of Tracilla's bedroom, she finally allowed herself a few hours of rest. She arose after that short rest driven with the urgency of a madwoman. She dressed herself quickly, giving orders to the harried handmaidens who were trying to meet her every need. She left the house as a whirlwind leaves the last place it has totally destroyed. The handmaidens breathed a sigh of relief while Tracilla's remaining child looked on with the loneliness and heartache no child should ever experience.

She immediately went to Farah's house to share her evil agenda with her old alliance. Farah was trying to prepare a meal for her husband and children. When Tracilla entered the house, she immediately left her duties to her husband and went with Tracilla to a far room in her home. As Tracilla told Farah what she planned to do, even Farah began to worry about the maliciousness they were about to indulge in. Tracilla was not going to go behind the scenes any longer. She was planning to openly attack the young man and his followers. Farah and Tracilla were well known in the area. Farah was afraid that some of Tracilla's shenanigans would hurt her standing in the community. Farah still believed she was well thought of in the surrounding homes. Little did she know people laughed at her behind her back. If Farah had known she would have been devastated.

Tracilla felt she was on a divine mission and anything she did would be upheld by the council. No one would dare go against them. When Farah objected to parts of her plan, Tracilla instantly admonished Farah for caring more for her reputation than for the future of the whole Jewish lineage. She knew exactly the words to calm Farah's worries. She knew how to reach inside the ego of the silly woman and stroke it to the point she would jump off a cliff for the admiration of Tracilla.

Tracilla knew her idea would have to be planned to the very smallest detail. She told Farah to stay close to home for the next week. They would use her home to practice and work out any kinks to the scenario they were planning. Farah agreed that Philibus would take the children out somewhere everyday so they would not be disturbed. Surely Philibus would not be an impediment to such a divine calling. Farah was shaking her head in agreement to Tracilla while in her mind she was devising how she could pick a fight with Philibus that night so he would take the children and go to his

SHEILA WILSON

mother's home. Such a divine plan built on lies, anger, jealousy and deviousness. Still these simple women could not see the error of their ways or even if they could, I don't think they would have turned away, so caught up in the thrill and power of it all.

CHAPTER 27

Mark 9:2-32 King James Version (KJV)

2 And after six days Jesus taketh with him Peter, and James, and John, and leadeth them up into an high mountain apart by themselves: and he was transfigured before them.

3 And his raiment became shining, exceeding white as snow; so as no fuller on earth can white them.

4 And there appeared unto them Elias with Moses: and they were talking with Jesus.

5 And Peter answered and said to Jesus, Master, it is good for us to be here: and let us make three tabernacles; one for thee, and one for Moses, and one for Elias.

6 For he wist not what to say; for they were sore afraid.

7 And there was a cloud that overshadowed them: and a voice came out of the cloud, saying, This is my beloved Son: hear him.

8 And suddenly, when they had looked round about, they saw no man any more, save Jesus only with themselves.

9 And as they came down from the mountain, he charged them that they should tell no man what things they had seen, till the Son of man were risen from the dead.

10 And they kept that saying with themselves, questioning one with another what the rising from the dead should mean.

11 And they asked him, saying, Why say the scribes that Elias must first come?

12 And he answered and told them, Elias verily cometh first, and restoreth all things; and how it is written of the Son of man, that he must suffer many things, and be set at nought.

13 But I say unto you, That Elias is indeed come, and they have done unto him whatsoever they listed, as it is written of him.

14 And when he came to his disciples, he saw a great multitude about them, and the scribes questioning with them.

15 And straightway all the people, when they beheld him, were greatly amazed, and running to him saluted him.

16 And he asked the scribes, What question ye with them?

17 And one of the multitude answered and said, Master, I have brought unto thee my son, which hath a dumb spirit;

18 And wheresoever he taketh him, he teareth him: and he foameth, and gnasheth with his teeth, and pineth away: and I spake to thy disciples that they should cast him out; and they could not.

19 He answereth him, and saith, O faithless generation, how long shall I be with you? how long shall I suffer you? bring him unto me.

20 And they brought him unto him: and when he saw him, straightway the spirit tare him; and he fell on the ground, and wallowed foaming.

21 And he asked his father, How long is it ago since this came unto him? And he said, Of a child.

22 And ofttimes it hath cast him into the fire, and into the waters, to destroy him: but if thou canst do any thing, have compassion on us, and help us.

23 Jesus said unto him, If thou canst believe, all things are possible to him that believeth.

24 And straightway the father of the child cried out, and said with tears, Lord, I believe; help thou mine unbelief.

25 When Jesus saw that the people came running together, he rebuked the foul spirit, saying unto him, Thou dumb and deaf spirit, I charge thee, come out of him, and enter no more into him.

26 And the spirit cried, and rent him sore, and came out of him: and he was as one dead; insomuch that many said, He is dead.

27 But Jesus took him by the hand, and lifted him up; and he arose.

28 And when he was come into the house, his disciples asked him privately, Why could not we cast him out?

29 And he said unto them, This kind can come forth by nothing, but by prayer and fasting.

30 And they departed thence, and passed through Galilee; and he would not that any man should know it.

31 For he taught his disciples, and said unto them, The Son of man is delivered into the hands of men, and they shall kill him; and after that he is killed, he shall rise the third day.

32 But they understood not that saying, and were afraid to ask him.

CHAPTER 28

For one whole week Tracilla and Farah practiced their deception in the confines of Farah's meager home. By the end of the week Farah had come to believe they were really on some type of divine calling. She had convinced herself of this because of the horrible treatment she had dealt to Philibus to get him out of the house for the week. She knew she could possibly have crossed the line because this time she had attacked his very manhood. Philibus had gathered the children and left the house in a rage saying things to Farah he would not have dared to say in the past. Throughout the week Farah had been planning a way to win her husband back when this was all over. She dared not tell Tracilla what had happened as she knew it would be all over the town before nightfall. She simply told Tracilla, Philibus had agreed to spend the week at his mother's home because he knew of the importance of their mission.

Tracilla had been keeping her ears and eyes open to any morsel of information she could get about the preacher man. She had heard he had performed some type of miracle in a nearby region. The people had been overwhelmed at what happened but puzzled because of the failure of his very own followers, who could not perform the same miracle yet were performing others around the land. Tracilla was quite pleased about this information because it seemed to be setting the stage for what she and Farah had planned.

Tracilla and Farah agreed to meet the next morning with the council to inform them of their plan. Tracilla felt it would be more believable if the council were present. Tracilla bid farewell to her partner and began the long walk to her home. She had found these long walks were ideal times to listen to the voices in her head. Even though sometimes she felt an uneasiness as they rambled on becoming more guttural and evil.

Micah and their remaining child were eating the evening meal as she entered the home. They knew to keep quiet until Tracilla spoke or they risked being the recipient of her returning razor like tongue. This evening Tracilla passed by them as if they did not exist. She had become so intent on her evil purpose that their presence had become an annoyance and now she simply dismissed them as unimportant details in her life. Micah had long ago gotten over the hurt at such slights. He now just endured her presence. Tracilla would have been outraged if she had known the true feelings of her husband. Her child had come to accept the fact his mother was not like all of the other mothers in the region. As he was growing older, he was making choices in his small mind to either model his mother's behavior or to reject everything she had ever taught or lived in front of him. Tracilla was losing the most important people in her life and she didn't realize or didn't care that it was happening.

Early the next morning Tracilla dressed in her most expensive and impressive clothes. She did not want to blend into the crowd on this most important day. She had told Farah to do the same but she was very apprehensive of what she would wear. Farah's taste in clothing had a lot to be desired as far as Tracilla was concerned. She hurried to Farah's home to find her laying on her bed crying beyond reason. She tried to make her friend tell her what was wrong but was only met with unintelligible sounds. She ran to get a bowl of water and washed Farah's face trying to get her to calm down. When Farah finally calmed down enough to speak, Tracilla was enraged by what her friend said.

"Tracilla, you must forgive me. I will not be able to accompany you today. Philibus has returned home and given me an ultimatum. I must remain home and care for the children or he will leave me forever. He came early this morning without the children to tell me this. He has returned to get the children. I am so sorry but you must go alone." Farah said.

"What! You know how important this is. You can't possibly desert me now. I need your help, Farah. We have planned this all week. The future of the Jewish nation rests on you and me. You can't possibly mean to tell me your family would be more important than that. This is ridiculous. Get your clothes on. You are coming with me." With this Tracilla dismissed the very core of human civilization as trivial, the family. She began to gather Farah's clothes realizing with all that had happened they would not be able to make it to the meeting with the council. Tracilla sent a message asking for forgiveness in this and would report the day's accomplishments later.

Farah wailed as she put her clothes on knowing when she returned she would never see her family again. She begged Tracilla to have mercy on her and her family. Tracilla ignored her pleadings and admonished her for putting her family above the Lord's business. She threatened Farah with ruin if she did not go. Farah was torn because she knew Philibus had meant what he said. If she went with Tracilla she would be left alone and destitute. If she didn't she would be Tracilla's latest target for destruction. She finally realized she had worked herself into a position of doom on both sides. Farah was completely devastated because in the past she had always had a way of escape. Today she had none.

CHAPTER 29

Mark 9:33-50 King James Version (KJV)

33 And he came to Capernaum: and being in the house he asked them, What was it that ye disputed among yourselves by the way?

34 But they held their peace: for by the way they had disputed among themselves, who should be the greatest.

35 And he sat down, and called the twelve, and saith unto them, If any man desire to be first, the same shall be last of all, and servant of all.

36 And he took a child, and set him in the midst of them: and when he had taken him in his arms, he said unto them,

37 Whosoever shall receive one of such children in my name, receiveth me: and whosoever shall receive me, receiveth not me, but him that sent me.

38 And John answered him, saying, Master, we saw one casting out devils in thy name, and he followeth not us: and we forbad him, because he followeth not us.

39 But Jesus said, Forbid him not: for there is no man which shall do a miracle in my name, that can lightly speak evil of me.

40 For he that is not against us is on our part.

41 For whosoever shall give you a cup of water to drink in my name, because ye belong to Christ, verily I say unto you, he shall not lose his reward.

42 And whosoever shall offend one of these little ones that believe in me, it is better for him that a millstone were hanged about his neck, and he were cast into the sea.

43 And if thy hand offend thee, cut it off: it is better for thee to enter into life maimed, than having two hands to go into hell, into the fire that never shall be quenched:

44 Where their worm dieth not, and the fire is not quenched.

45 And if thy foot offend thee, cut it off: it is better for thee to enter halt into life, than having two feet to be cast into hell, into the fire that never shall be quenched:

46 Where their worm dieth not, and the fire is not quenched.

47 And if thine eye offend thee, pluck it out: it is better for thee to enter into the kingdom of God with one eye, than having two eyes to be cast into hell fire:

48 Where their worm dieth not, and the fire is not quenched.

49 For every one shall be salted with fire, and every sacrifice shall be salted with salt.

50 Salt is good: but if the salt have lost his saltness, wherewith will ye season it? Have salt in yourselves, and have peace one with another.

Mark 10:1-16 King James Version (KJV)

10 And he arose from thence, and cometh into the coasts of Judaea by the farther side of Jordan: and the people resort unto him again; and, as he was wont, he taught them again.

2 And the Pharisees came to him, and asked him, Is it lawful for a man to put away his wife? tempting him.

3 And he answered and said unto them, What did Moses command you?

4 And they said, Moses suffered to write a bill of divorcement, and to put her away.

5 And Jesus answered and said unto them, For the hardness of your heart he wrote you this precept.

6 But from the beginning of the creation God made them male and female.

7 For this cause shall a man leave his father and mother, and cleave to his wife;

8 And they twain shall be one flesh: so then they are no more twain, but one flesh.

9 What therefore God hath joined together, let not man put asunder.

10 And in the house his disciples asked him again of the same matter.

11 And he saith unto them, Whosoever shall put away his wife, and marry another, committeth adultery against her.

12 And if a woman shall put away her husband, and be married to another, she committeth adultery.

13 And they brought young children to him, that he should touch them: and his disciples rebuked those that brought them.

14 But when Jesus saw it, he was much displeased, and said unto them, Suffer the little children to come unto me, and forbid them not: for of such is the kingdom of God.

15 Verily I say unto you, Whosoever shall not receive the kingdom of God as a little child, he shall not enter therein.

16 And he took them up in his arms, put his hands upon them, and blessed them.

In the crowd two vipers were watching Jesus as he blessed the children. A rage came over Tracilla as she watched this and she clutched Farah's arm until Farah openly wailed at the pain. Tracilla knew the time was ripe but she had misgivings about Farah. She decided she would just have to continue on with the plan and hope Farah would collect herself enough to be effective.

CHAPTER 30

Tracilla and Farrah followed at a safe distance behind Jesus and the crowd.

Mark 10:17-31 King James Version (KJV)

17 And when he was gone forth into the way, there came one running, and kneeled to him, and asked him, Good Master, what shall I do that I may inherit eternal life?

18 And Jesus said unto him, Why callest thou me good? there is none good but one, that is, God.

19 Thou knowest the commandments, Do not commit adultery, Do not kill, Do not steal, Do not bear false witness, Defraud not, Honour thy father and mother.

20 And he answered and said unto him, Master, all these have I observed from my youth.

21 Then Jesus beholding him loved him, and said unto him, One thing thou lackest: go thy way, sell whatsoever thou hast, and give to the poor, and thou shalt have treasure in heaven: and come, take up the cross, and follow me.

22 And he was sad at that saying, and went away grieved: for he had great possessions.

23 And Jesus looked round about, and saith unto his disciples, How hardly shall they that have riches enter into the kingdom of God!

24 And the disciples were astonished at his words. But Jesus answereth again, and saith unto them, Children, how hard is it for them that trust in riches to enter into the kingdom of God!

25 It is easier for a camel to go through the eye of a needle, than for a rich man to enter into the kingdom of God.

26 And they were astonished out of measure, saying among themselves, Who then can be saved?

27 And Jesus looking upon them saith, With men it is impossible, but not with God: for with God all things are possible.

28 Then Peter began to say unto him, Lo, we have left all, and have followed thee.

29 And Jesus answered and said, Verily I say unto you, There is no man that hath left house, or brethren, or sisters, or father, or mother, or wife, or children, or lands, for my sake, and the gospel's,

30 But he shall receive an hundredfold now in this time, houses, and brethren, and sisters, and mothers, and children, and lands, with persecutions; and in the world to come eternal life.

31 But many that are first shall be last; and the last first.

As Jesus spoke the last sentence, Tracilla launched into a tirade against the man of Galilee. She began to rant and rave how he was a fraud. Putting on her most dramatic look, Tracilla began to tell the crowds on the road how this man had caused the death of her child and had crippled her most dear friend. With this she waved her arm toward Farah, who was suppose to twist her body in a painful, deformed manner. Farah had done this, but what the crowd did not realize was that the tears falling from her eyes were not the result of the physical pain, but from the emotional emptiness in her heart.

"This man had his 'cohorts in deception' feed my precious child poison which resulted in an agonizing death for her and unending grief for me and her father. She was one of the ones he bids unto him. He pretends to show so much caring and love for them, but it is all a ruse. A deception to cloud your minds so you can not see his ultimate goal of control and power. He is a monster preying upon the very souls of your children."

As Tracilla continued, Jesus stood and looked at her with such compassion, many of the people in the crowd were moved into undying allegiance to him. They realized only a supernatural nature could look at this raving maniac with such love. They became believers because of Jesus' reaction to Tracilla's hate. How many people have been saved because of a person's reaction to cruelty and mockery?

When Tracilla saw she was losing the crowd because of Jesus' nonreaction to her, she decided to change her tactics. She pulled Farah from the side of the road and implored the crowd to look at her dear friend. "She was able to move freely a few days before until she was at a healing meeting of Jesus. At this meeting one of his so called disciples tripped my good friend, causing her to stumble into a massive hole in the road. The disciples then dragged her to their master who supposedly healed her with the laying on of his hands. They then told her family members to carry her home so she could rest from all the excitement. They did as they were told and the next morning Farah's back was twisted so that walking is excruciatingly painful and to sit straight is impossible. Everyday the pain is becoming worse and her deformity more pronounced. This is not healing, this is trickery. Listen, my good friends, we can not let this man hurt anyone else. He is a menace to our beliefs and families."

Jesus still stood quietly and serenely as Tracilla cast her accusations at him and his followers. His followers were becoming quite angry at the aspersions spouted at them. They could not understand how Jesus could stand calmly by as such lies were being said against him and themselves. Sometimes seeing the complete picture can cause a calmness of the spirit which is unearthly. I wonder if we humbled ourselves enough if the Lord would give us a peak at the fullness of it all and I wonder how many people would be saved if we would only let him show us?

Tracilla was giving her ultimate performance but something was terribly wrong. The people were not rallying with her. In fact they seemed to be stepping back so no one would even be remotely associated with her. The more she ranted and raved, the more the people backed away. Tracilla felt she was losing control and it was a feeling she did not like. She looked at the man standing before her and instead of hate and anger, she was met with the most profound stare of love and understanding she had ever encountered. This she could not bare. She immediately lowered her head and grabbing Farah began to run back down the road. Something had gone terribly wrong and she couldn't figure it out. Her plan was to ridicule and expose the man as a liar and a fraud, but in fact the opposite had happened. The people were more drawn to him than ever.

She noticed people looking and staring at her as she hurried home. She then realized how she must look. She was still ranting and raving, with no one around her. Farah was following close behind and when she turned to look she was horrified. Because instead of dressing Farah in clothes that would impress and intimidate, she saw she had dressed Farah in her oldest clothes which had holes and spots on them. She then looked down at her own attire and found she was dressed in the same manner. She thought she had been so careful to dress herself and Farah so there would be no mistake of what class they were from. What had happened? Who had played this horrible joke on the two women? They both looked and sounded like babbling idiots.

CHAPTER 31

After the confrontation with the two women:

Mark 10:32-52 King James Version (KJV)

32 And they were in the way going up to Jerusalem; and Jesus went before them: and they were amazed; and as they followed, they were afraid. And he took again the twelve, and began to tell them what things should happen unto him,

33 Saying, Behold, we go up to Jerusalem; and the Son of man shall be delivered unto the chief priests, and unto the scribes; and they shall condemn him to death, and shall deliver him to the Gentiles:

34 And they shall mock him, and shall scourge him, and shall spit upon him, and shall kill him: and the third day he shall rise again.

35 And James and John, the sons of Zebedee, come unto him, saying, Master, we would that thou shouldest do for us whatsoever we shall desire.

36 And he said unto them, What would ye that I should do for you?

37 They said unto him, Grant unto us that we may sit, one on thy right hand, and the other on thy left hand, in thy glory.

38 But Jesus said unto them, Ye know not what ye ask: can ye drink of the cup that I drink of? and be baptized with the baptism that I am baptized with?

39 And they said unto him, We can. And Jesus said unto them, Ye shall indeed drink of the cup that I drink of; and with the baptism that I am baptized withal shall ye be baptized:

40 But to sit on my right hand and on my left hand is not mine to give; but it shall be given to them for whom it is prepared.

41 And when the ten heard it, they began to be much displeased with James and John.

42 But Jesus called them to him, and saith unto them, Ye know that they which are accounted to rule over the Gentiles exercise lordship over them; and their great ones exercise authority upon them.

43 But so shall it not be among you: but whosoever will be great among you, shall be your minister:

44 And whosoever of you will be the chiefest, shall be servant of all.

45 For even the Son of man came not to be ministered unto, but to minister, and to give his life a ransom for many.

46 And they came to Jericho: and as he went out of Jericho with his disciples and a great number of people, blind Bartimaeus, the son of Timaeus, sat by the highway side begging.

47 And when he heard that it was Jesus of Nazareth, he began to cry out, and say, Jesus, thou son of David, have mercy on me.

48 And many charged him that he should hold his peace: but he cried the more a great deal, Thou son of David, have mercy on me.

49 And Jesus stood still, and commanded him to be called. And they call the blind man, saying unto him, Be of good comfort, rise; he calleth thee.

50 And he, casting away his garment, rose, and came to Jesus.

51 And Jesus answered and said unto him, What wilt thou that I should do unto thee? The blind man said unto him, Lord, that I might receive my sight.

52 And Jesus said unto him, Go thy way; thy faith hath made thee whole. And immediately he received his sight, and followed Jesus in the way.

Mark 11:1-11 King James Version (KJV)

1 And when they came nigh to Jerusalem, unto Bethphage and Bethany, at the mount of Olives, he sendeth forth two of his disciples,

2 And saith unto them, Go your way into the village over against you: and as soon as ye be entered into it, ye shall find a colt tied, whereon never man sat; loose him, and bring him.

3 And if any man say unto you, Why do ye this? say ye that the Lord hath need of him; and straightway he will send him hither.

4 And they went their way, and found the colt tied by the door without in a place where two ways met; and they loose him.

5 And certain of them that stood there said unto them, What do ye, loosing the colt?

6 And they said unto them even as Jesus had commanded: and they let them go.

7 And they brought the colt to Jesus, and cast their garments on him; and he sat upon him.

8 And many spread their garments in the way: and others cut down branches off the trees, and strawed them in the way.

9 And they that went before, and they that followed, cried, saying, Hosanna; Blessed is he that cometh in the name of the Lord:

10 Blessed be the kingdom of our father David, that cometh in the name of the Lord: Hosanna in the highest.

11 And Jesus entered into Jerusalem, and into the temple: and when he had looked round about upon all things, and now the eventide was come, he went out unto Bethany with the twelve.

CHAPTER 32

Tracilla and Farah hurried home after making spectacles of themselves. Tracilla was in complete confusion. Her confidence was shattered and for some reason she felt betrayed but she couldn't understand why. All the way home the voices in her head had turned to ridiculing laughter. She tried to shut them out by covering her ears but this only made them louder and more forceful. She was finally realizing these voices were not from this world but from some dark part which she was now a part of.

When they reached Farah's home they were met with an unnatural quietness. Farah rushed through her home to find many belongings missing. She flung herself upon the floor when she realized Philibus had made good his threat. He had left her alone and desolate. Farah kept imploring of Tracilla what she should do. Tracilla could only answer her with unintelligible garble. The confusion was incapacitating her physically and mentally. She left Farah in her empty house and rushed home to find some type of normalcy which she was desperate to be a part of.

Tracilla began to run down the road toward her home, trying to outrun the voices which had become inhuman. They were now attacking her, telling her she was stupid, a fool, a pawn in the devil's game. As she entered her house, she was screaming at the top of her lungs, "No, No, No, You are a liar!" To this the voices began laughing again saying, "Now you understand, I am the Father of Lies and you are all mine."

Tracilla's son was so frightened by the appearance of his mother, he ran screaming to the back of the house. Tracilla followed him only to run into Micah who was trying to comfort his young son. Tracilla lunged for the boy but Micah stopped her.

"Tracilla, compose yourself. You are terrifying the boy. Look at yourself. What have you been doing all day? You are a horrible sight. Don't tell me you went out in public looking as you do! You look like someone who has lost their mind!"

Micah spoke harshly to Tracilla. Gone were the loving tones he used with his wife. Micah had come to the conclusion their relationship was totally over. When he looked at her it was with a look of disgust. He would not throw her out. Not because she didn't deserve it, but because this was something he could not do to his only remaining child. Children always seem to bear the sins of their parents.

Looking at her husband and child, Tracilla suddenly realized what she had lost in the last few years. She knew there was nothing she could do or say to recapture the love which was now gone. With horror, her eyes were open to the pain, loneliness and heartache she had caused the ones which were suppose to be dearest to her. She ran from the room to the garden and began to weep the tears of a thousand heartaches. Her sobs could be heard all through the night, yet no one would dare go to the garden to comfort her. They simply did not care.

CHAPTER 33

Mark 11:12-33 King James Version (KJV)

12 And on the morrow, when they were come from Bethany, he was hungry:

13 And seeing a fig tree afar off having leaves, he came, if haply he might find any thing thereon: and when he came to it, he found nothing but leaves; for the time of figs was not yet.

14 And Jesus answered and said unto it, No man eat fruit of thee hereafter for ever. And his disciples heard it.

15 And they come to Jerusalem: and Jesus went into the temple, and began to cast out them that sold and bought in the temple, and overthrew the tables of the moneychangers, and the seats of them that sold doves;

16 And would not suffer that any man should carry any vessel through the temple.

17 And he taught, saying unto them, Is it not written, My house shall be called of all nations the house of prayer? but ye have made it a den of thieves.

18 And the scribes and chief priests heard it, and sought how they might destroy him: for they feared him, because all the people was astonished at his doctrine.

19 And when even was come, he went out of the city.

20 And in the morning, as they passed by, they saw the fig tree dried up from the roots.

21 And Peter calling to remembrance saith unto him, Master, behold, the fig tree which thou cursedst is withered away.

22 And Jesus answering saith unto them, Have faith in God.

23 For verily I say unto you, That whosoever shall say unto this mountain, Be thou removed, and be thou cast into the sea; and shall not doubt in his heart, but shall believe that those things which he saith shall come to pass; he shall have whatsoever he saith.

24 Therefore I say unto you, What things soever ye desire, when ye pray, believe that ye receive them, and ye shall have them.

25 And when ye stand praying, forgive, if ye have ought against any: that your Father also which is in heaven may forgive you your trespasses.

26 But if ye do not forgive, neither will your Father which is in heaven forgive your trespasses.

27 And they come again to Jerusalem: and as he was walking in the temple, there come to him the chief priests, and the scribes, and the elders,

28 And say unto him, By what authority doest thou these things? and who gave thee this authority to do these things?

29 And Jesus answered and said unto them, I will also ask of you one question, and answer me, and I will tell you by what authority I do these things.

30 The baptism of John, was it from heaven, or of men? answer me.

31 And they reasoned with themselves, saying, If we shall say, From heaven; he will say, Why then did ye not believe him?

32 But if we shall say, Of men; they feared the people: for all men counted John, that he was a prophet indeed.

33 And they answered and said unto Jesus, We cannot tell. And Jesus answering saith unto them, Neither do I tell you by what authority I do these things.

Mark 12:1-12 King James Version (KJV)

12 And he began to speak unto them by parables. A certain man planted a vineyard, and set an hedge about it, and digged a place for the winefat, and built a tower, and let it out to husbandmen, and went into a far country.

2 And at the season he sent to the husbandmen a servant, that he might receive from the husbandmen of the fruit of the vineyard.

3 And they caught him, and beat him, and sent him away empty.

4 And again he sent unto them another servant; and at him they cast stones, and wounded him in the head, and sent him away shamefully handled.

5 And again he sent another; and him they killed, and many others; beating some, and killing some.

6 Having yet therefore one son, his wellbeloved, he sent him also last unto them, saying, They will reverence my son.

7 But those husbandmen said among themselves, This is the heir; come, let us kill him, and the inheritance shall be ours.'

8 And they took him, and killed him, and cast him out of the vineyard.

9 What shall therefore the lord of the vineyard do? he will come and destroy the husbandmen, and will give the vineyard unto others.

10 And have ye not read this scripture; The stone which the builders rejected is become the head of the corner:

11 This was the Lord's doing, and it is marvelous in our eyes?

12 And they sought to lay hold on him, but feared the people: for they knew that he had spoken the parable against them: and they left him, and went their way.

CHAPTER 34

The religious authority of the time had never been more perplexed and at odds. This young man could baffle them with the simplest questions. They knew something must be done as this man was going to cause an insurrection among the people. The people were beginning to wonder why the chief priests and teachers of the law had no answer to his parables which were so obviously against them. These men did not want to lose their positions of authority and favor within the Jewish and Roman community. This meant much more to them than even serving the most Holy God.

They met the next day to discuss what could be done to hasten his arrest. The people were not succumbing to all of the blatant lies and rumors which they had been spreading. In fact the only thing they had heard the people say against the preacher man was a question of his birth and lowly upbringing. This seemed to disturb the people more than all of the religious arguments which they had presented to the young man. They had no idea where that rumor had started or even if it were true.

Later that day, while still discussing the matter, they were surprised with a visit from their favored rumormonger, Tracilla. They were all shocked at her appearance. She was disheveled and wild eyed. Her hair had not been brushed and her face was red and puffy. She did not wait to be announced. She was desperate to see approving looks, but what she got were looks of disgust and revulsion. She tried to hold herself upright and look at them with an air of confidence and superiority, but for some reason all of her self confidence was lost in the guttural sounds of the voices in her head.

She tried to impress them with stories of triumph over Jesus and his followers, but even Tracilla's gift of persuasion was lost and her stories came out pitiful and vain. The religious leaders were appalled by her all around appearance and presentation. Right in front of her they made the decision to cut all of their ties with the wayward, lost soul. Tracilla was devastated. She knew this was the death blow to her visions of power and glory. She begged the leaders to give her another chance. She would do better in her quest.

They told her she would not be needed any longer and not to disturb their meetings ever again. Mosha took great delight in telling her she had accomplished nothing, that someone else had started a better rumor with evidently just a whisper in the right ears. He then proceeded to tell her of the people's disturbance of Jesus' conception and birth.

Tracilla could not believe what she was hearing. She was hearing exactly what she had spoken years ago on the side of the Jordan River. Words which had tripped so easily and lightly out of her mouth. Words spoken in low and whispered tones to the group of women gathered along the banks watching the young man's baptism. As Mosha spoke, the realization of what she was hearing sank in. Tracilla first began to giggle, then she began laughing so hard she could not stand upright. All of the leaders looked on at the obviously mad woman. They motioned for the guards to remove her and all agreed she was to be banned from the temple courts forever. They could not be associated with someone with such an obvious mental disturbance.

All the way home Tracilla laughed and cried. She had lost everything to destroy this man called Jesus when 'Just a Whisper' was all it took. Just a whisper of innuendo about something she had no knowledge about. Just a whisper in the right ears. Just a whisper was all it took to set the hounds of propriety after you. She had lost her husband, her family, her wealth, her beauty, her social standing, her influence when all it really took was 'Just a Whisper'.

After Tracilla left, the religious leaders decided to send others in to try and trap Jesus.

CHAPTER 35

Mark 12:13-44 King James Version (KJV)

13 And they send unto him certain of the Pharisees and of the Herodians, to catch him in his words.

14 And when they were come, they say unto him, Master, we know that thou art true, and carest for no man: for thou regardest not the person of men, but teachest the way of God in truth: Is it lawful to give tribute to Caesar, or not?

15 Shall we give, or shall we not give? But he, knowing their hypocrisy, said unto them, Why tempt ye me? bring me a penny, that I may see it.

16 And they brought it. And he saith unto them, Whose is this image and superscription? And they said unto him, Caesar's.

17 And Jesus answering said unto them, Render to Caesar the things that are Caesar's, and to God the things that are God's. And they marvelled at him.

18 Then come unto him the Sadducees, which say there is no resurrection; and they asked him, saying,

19 Master, Moses wrote unto us, If a man's brother die, and leave his wife behind him, and leave no children, that his brother should take his wife, and raise up seed unto his brother.

20 Now there were seven brethren: and the first took a wife, and dying left no seed.

21 And the second took her, and died, neither left he any seed: and the third likewise.

22 And the seven had her, and left no seed: last of all the woman died also.

23 In the resurrection therefore, when they shall rise, whose wife shall she be of them? for the seven had her to wife.

24 And Jesus answering said unto them, Do ye not therefore err, because ye know not the scriptures, neither the power of God?

25 For when they shall rise from the dead, they neither marry, nor are given in marriage; but are as the angels which are in heaven.

26 And as touching the dead, that they rise: have ye not read in the book of Moses, how in the bush God spake unto him, saying, I am the God of Abraham, and the God of Isaac, and the God of Jacob?

27 He is not the God of the dead, but the God of the living: ye therefore do greatly err.

28 And one of the scribes came, and having heard them reasoning together, and perceiving that he had answered them well, asked him, Which is the first commandment of all?

29 And Jesus answered him, The first of all the commandments is, Hear, O Israel; The Lord our God is one Lord:

30 And thou shalt love the Lord thy God with all thy heart, and with all thy soul, and with all thy mind, and with all thy strength: this is the first commandment.

31 And the second is like, namely this, Thou shalt love thy neighbour as thyself. There is none other commandment greater than these.

32 And the scribe said unto him, Well, Master, thou hast said the truth: for there is one God; and there is none other but he:

33 And to love him with all the heart, and with all the understanding, and with all the soul, and with all the strength, and to love his neighbour as himself, is more than all whole burnt offerings and sacrifices.

34 And when Jesus saw that he answered discreetly, he said unto him, Thou art not far from the kingdom of God. And no man after that durst ask him any question.

CHAPTER 36

The teachers of the law were in total confusion at this time. Some were angry at the obvious contempt Jesus had for them while others had been questioning in their hearts many of the points he was bringing out. They all agreed the question and answer sessions were not accomplishing anything. In fact every time they attempted to confuse the young man he turned it around and baffled them. They all came to the conclusion this was a highly intelligent and learned man, yet they knew something had to be done or the easy lives they had been living would be disrupted and they could not have that happen.

They had lost all faith in Tracilla and her cohorts. Tracilla was now seen walking the streets in rags babbling to anyone who would listen to her, which was not many people as most were afraid of her. The ones who dared listen to her, did so out of pity or wanting to make fun of her in front of their friends.

Patisha took great pleasure in addressing Tracilla frequently in large groups. With her insincere sincerity, Patisha feigned concern for Tracilla and asked how she was doing. When Tracilla would begin babbling, Patisha would make a point of cutting her eyes to her friends and making exaggerated gestures which would send the silly flock of women into gales of laughter. In Tracilla's warped mind she thought Patisha was making jokes she did not understand to make her feel better. She never caught on that Patisha had become more corrupt than she had ever thought of being and was using her as the focal point of her levity.

The only person who truly reached out to Tracilla in kindness was Kasha. Even though she realized the evil Tracilla had perpetrated, her kind heart would not let her take advantage of anyone who was so down in their life. With Kasha, Tracilla would cry and try to make sense of what had happened to her and her family. Kasha, who had become a believer, would gently try to point Tracilla to the gentle man of Galilee. She tried to persuade Tracilla to go to him and bear her soul. Even in Tracilla's downtrodden state, she would not even consider humbling herself to such an extent. Kasha would kiss her friend and leave her to her ramblings.

Tracilla's son pretended she did not exist and Micah only acknowledged her when he wanted her to do something. Tracilla kept the house and cooked the meals. She tried to reach out to them by providing all of their creature comforts. They simply ignored her. If she began talking, one or both of them would simply leave the room. When her sobs were heard in the night, no one went to comfort her.

When Tracilla's misery became unbearable, she agreed to go with Kasha to hear the master speak. Tracilla would only go if Kasha agreed to stay in the back of the crowd and not get close to Jesus or any of his disciples.

CHAPTER 37

Mark 12:35-44 King James Version (KJV)

35 And Jesus answered and said, while he taught in the temple, How say the scribes that Christ is the son of David?

36 For David himself said by the Holy Ghost, The LORD said to my Lord, Sit thou on my right hand, till I make thine enemies thy footstool.

37 David therefore himself calleth him Lord; and whence is he then his son? And the common people heard him gladly.

38 And he said unto them in his doctrine, Beware of the scribes, which love to go in long clothing, and love salutations in the marketplaces,

39 And the chief seats in the synagogues, and the uppermost rooms at feasts:

40 Which devour widows' houses, and for a pretence make long prayers: these shall receive greater damnation.

41 And Jesus sat over against the treasury, and beheld how the people cast money into the treasury: and many that were rich cast in much.

42 And there came a certain poor widow, and she threw in two mites, which make a farthing.

43 And he called unto him his disciples, and saith unto them, Verily I say unto you, That this poor widow hath cast more in, than all they which have cast into the treasury:

44 For all they did cast in of their abundance; but she of her want did cast in all that she had, even all her living.

Mark 13 King James Version (KJV)

1 And as he went out of the temple, one of his disciples saith unto him, Master, see what manner of stones and what buildings are here!

2 And Jesus answering said unto him, Seest thou these great buildings? there shall not be left one stone upon another, that shall not be thrown down.

3 And as he sat upon the mount of Olives over against the temple, Peter and James and John and Andrew asked him privately,

4 Tell us, when shall these things be? and what shall be the sign when all these things shall be fulfilled?

5 And Jesus answering them began to say, Take heed lest any man deceive you:

6 For many shall come in my name, saying, I am Christ; and shall deceive many.

7 And when ye shall hear of wars and rumours of wars, be ye not troubled: for such things must needs be; but the end shall not be yet.

8 For nation shall rise against nation, and kingdom against kingdom: and there shall be earthquakes in divers places, and there shall be famines and troubles: these are the beginnings of sorrows.

9 But take heed to yourselves: for they shall deliver you up to councils; and in the synagogues ye shall be beaten: and ye shall be brought before rulers and kings for my sake, for a testimony against them.

10 And the gospel must first be published among all nations.

11 But when they shall lead you, and deliver you up, take no thought beforehand what ye shall speak, neither do ye premeditate: but whatsoever shall be given you in that hour, that speak ye: for it is not ye that speak, but the Holy Ghost.

12 Now the brother shall betray the brother to death, and the father the son; and children shall rise up against their parents, and shall cause them to be put to death.

13 And ye shall be hated of all men for my name's sake: but he that shall endure unto the end, the same shall be saved.

14 But when ye shall see the abomination of desolation, spoken of by Daniel the prophet, standing where it ought not, (let him that readeth understand,) then let them that be in Judaea flee to the mountains:

15 And let him that is on the housetop not go down into the house, neither enter therein, to take any thing out of his house:

16 And let him that is in the field not turn back again for to take up his garment.

17 But woe to them that are with child, and to them that give suck in those days!

18 And pray ye that your flight be not in the winter.

19 For in those days shall be affliction, such as was not from the beginning of the creation which God created unto this time, neither shall be.

20 And except that the Lord had shortened those days, no flesh should be saved: but for the elect's sake, whom he hath chosen, he hath shortened the days.

21 And then if any man shall say to you, Lo, here is Christ; or, lo, he is there; believe him not:

22 For false Christs and false prophets shall rise, and shall shew signs and wonders, to seduce, if it were possible, even the elect.

23 But take ye heed: behold, I have foretold you all things.

24 But in those days, after that tribulation, the sun shall be darkened, and the moon shall not give her light,

25 And the stars of heaven shall fall, and the powers that are in heaven shall be shaken.

26 And then shall they see the Son of man coming in the clouds with great power and glory.

27 And then shall he send his angels, and shall gather together his elect from the four winds, from the uttermost part of the earth to the uttermost part of heaven.

28 Now learn a parable of the fig tree; When her branch is yet tender, and putteth forth leaves, ye know that summer is near:

29 So ye in like manner, when ye shall see these things come to pass, know that it is nigh, even at the doors.

30 Verily I say unto you, that this generation shall not pass, till all these things be done.

31 Heaven and earth shall pass away: but my words shall not pass away.

32 But of that day and that hour knoweth no man, no, not the angels which are in heaven, neither the Son, but the Father.

33 Take ye heed, watch and pray: for ye know not when the time is.

34 For the Son of Man is as a man taking a far journey, who left his house, and gave authority to his servants, and to every man his work, and commanded the porter to watch.

35 Watch ye therefore: for ye know not when the master of the house cometh, at even, or at midnight, or at the cockcrowing, or in the morning:

36 Lest coming suddenly he find you sleeping.

37 And what I say unto you I say unto all, Watch!

CHAPTER 38

Tracilla's misery grew heavier and heavier each day. Going to hear Jesus with Kasha only compounded her feelings of worthlessness and guilt. She could not eat or sleep. She walked around in a daze automatically performing the duties of each day. People shunned her, so no one realized the depths to which Tracilla was falling. Loving your neighbor as you love yourself was only practiced by Kasha. She checked on Tracilla daily searching for ways to lift her newfound friend out of her valley of despair.

Kasha encouraged Tracilla to go to Jesus and humbly submit herself for his healing. Tracilla would not go as she felt to be forgiven was impossible, especially from one she had castigated so. She drifted through life as a shell, devoid of any hope or comfort. Kasha was so burdened for Tracilla, she prayed for hours each day about her. Even though she received great comfort from these sessions with God, she could not see a change in her friend's outlook on life.

Farah came to see Tracilla once, but her vengeance was so apparent, Kasha rushed her along. Farah blamed Tracilla for all of her own woes. It was still impossible for her to look at herself as being at fault at all. Philibus had not returned and Farah's coffers were becoming very low. She besieged her friends, family, and even acquaintances for money and help. Many people took pity upon Farah, convinced she had been duped by the evil Tracilla. The pity would last until Farah began to hound them day in and day out for money. She would try to lay so much guilt on everyone else, she eventually scared everyone away from her. Her welcome to many prominent homes in the community had been closed because of her overbearing demands.

The gentle man of Galilee continued to travel the countryside preaching his good news of the coming of the Kingdom of God. Many people were saved because of the miracles, many because of the preaching and many more because of his reaction to people's open hostility and condemnation. He never struck back at these people. He only loved them with such intensity they soon hung their heads and receded back into the crowds. He loved through actions more than words which disturbed the religious leaders of the day. People were being drawn to him because he lived what he preached and preached what he lived. This was a new concept to the people who were use to laws, laws, and more laws. To be loved for themselves and not for what they did was a refreshing concept they were open to.

The savior changed many lives in the three short years of his ministry. Husbands began to love their wives and wives began to honor their husbands. Children were brought up in the way they should go and not on the whims of the emotions of their parents. People treated each other with a different attitude. You were not honored or respected for who you are, you were treated with honor and respect just because you are. Instead of jealousy of another's accomplishments, people began to feel joy for them. Each person's talents and possessions were appreciated, not coveted in the old way. People began to walk away from idle conversations and gossip. The people who continued to gossip found their audiences were becoming smaller and smaller. If a person wanted to know about you, he would go to you and strike up a conversation. People stopped relying on second hand information about people. Because of this, people became more open and trusting. Mistakes were not held over a person's head to beat him down whenever he tried to do better. Life was becoming more joyful for all people, not just a select few. These marvelous, yet treacherous, times had no effect on Tracilla who had begun the downfall of the wonderful minister with just a whisper.

CHAPTER 39

Mark 14:1-37 King James Version (KJV)

1 After two days was the feast of the passover, and of unleavened bread: and the chief priests and the scribes sought how they might take him by craft, and put him to death.

2 But they said, Not on the feast day, lest there be an uproar of the people.

3 And being in Bethany in the house of Simon the leper, as he sat at meat, there came a woman having an alabaster box of ointment of spikenard very precious; and she brake the box, and poured it on his head.

4 And there were some that had indignation within themselves, and said, Why was this waste of the ointment made?

5 For it might have been sold for more than three hundred pence, and have been given to the poor. And they murmured against her.

6 And Jesus said, Let her alone; why trouble ye her? she hath wrought a good work on me.

7 For ye have the poor with you always, and whensoever ye will ye may do them good: but me ye have not always.

8 She hath done what she could: she is come aforehand to anoint my body to the burying.

9 Verily I say unto you, Whersoever this gospel shall be preached throughout the whole world, this also that she hath done shall be spoken of for a memorial of her.

10 And Judas Iscariot, one of the twelve, went unto the chief priests, to betray him unto them.

11 And when they heard it, they were glad, and promised to give him money. And he sought how he might conveniently betray him.

12 And the first day of unleavened bread, when they killed the passover, his disciples said unto him, Where wilt thou that we go and prepare that thou mayest eat the passover?

13 And he sendeth forth two of his disciples, and saith unto them, Go ye into the city, and there shall meet you a man bearing a pitcher of water: follow him.

14 And wheresoever he shall go in, say ye to the goodman of the house, The Master saith, Where is the guestchamber, where I shall eat the passover with my disciples?

15 And he will shew you a large upper room furnished and prepared: there make ready for us.

16 And his disciples went forth, and came into the city, and found as he had said unto them: and they made ready the passover.

17 And in the evening he cometh with the twelve.

18 And as they sat and did eat, Jesus said, Verily I say unto you, One of you which eateth with me shall betray me.

19 And they began to be sorrowful, and to say unto him one by one, Is it I? and another said, Is it I?

20 And he answered and said unto them, It is one of the twelve, that dippeth with me in the dish.

21 The Son of man indeed goeth, as it is written of him: but woe to that man by whom the Son of man is betrayed! good were it for that man if he had never been born.

22 And as they did eat, Jesus took bread, and blessed, and brake it, and gave to them, and said, Take, eat: this is my body.

23 And he took the cup, and when he had given thanks, he gave it to them: and they all drank of it.

24 And he said unto them, This is my blood of the new testament, which is shed for many.

25 Verily I say unto you, I will drink no more of the fruit of the vine, until that day that I drink it new in the kingdom of God.

26 And when they had sung an hymn, they went out into the mount of Olives.

27 And Jesus saith unto them, All ye shall be offended because of me this night: for it is written, I will smite the shepherd, and the sheep shall be scattered.

28 But after that I am risen, I will go before you into Galilee.

29 But Peter said unto him, Although all shall be offended, yet will not I.

30 And Jesus saith unto him, Verily I say unto thee, That this day, even in this night, before the cock crow twice, thou shalt deny me thrice.

31 But he spake the more vehemently, If I should die with thee, I will not deny thee in any wise. Likewise also said they all.

32 And they came to a place which was named Gethsemane: and he saith to his disciples, Sit ye here, while I shall pray.

33 And he taketh with him Peter and James and John, and began to be sore amazed, and to be very heavy;

34 And saith unto them, My soul is exceeding sorrowful unto death: tarry ye here, and watch.

35 And he went forward a little, and fell on the ground, and prayed that, if it were possible, the hour might pass from him.

36 And he said, Abba, Father, all things are possible unto thee; take away this cup from me: nevertheless not what I will, but what thou wilt.

37 And he cometh, and findeth them sleeping, and saith unto Peter, Simon, sleepest thou? couldest not thou watch one hour?

Mark 14:38-72 King James Version (KJV)

38 Watch ye and pray, lest ye enter into temptation. The spirit truly is ready, but the flesh is weak.

39 And again he went away, and prayed, and spake the same words.

40 And when he returned, he found them asleep again, (for their eyes were heavy,) neither wist they what to answer him.

41 And he cometh the third time, and saith unto them, Sleep on now, and take your rest: it is enough, the hour is come; behold, the Son of man is betrayed into the hands of sinners.

42 Rise up, let us go; lo, he that betrayeth me is at hand.

43 And immediately, while he yet spake, cometh Judas, one of the twelve, and with him a great multitude with swords and staves, from the chief priests and the scribes and the elders.

44 And he that betrayed him had given them a token, saying, Whomsoever I shall kiss, that same is he; take him, and lead him away safely.

45 And as soon as he was come, he goeth straightway to him, and saith, Master, master; and kissed him.

46 And they laid their hands on him, and took him.

47 And one of them that stood by drew a sword, and smote a servant of the high priest, and cut off his ear.

48 And Jesus answered and said unto them, Are ye come out, as against a thief, with swords and with staves to take me?

49 I was daily with you in the temple teaching, and ye took me not: but the scriptures must be fulfilled.

50 And they all forsook him, and fled.

51 And there followed him a certain young man, having a linen cloth cast about his naked body; and the young men laid hold on him:

52 *And he left the linen cloth, and fled from them naked.*

53 *And they led Jesus away to the high priest: and with him were assembled all the chief priests and the elders and the scribes.*

54 *And Peter followed him afar off, even into the palace of the high priest: and he sat with the servants, and warmed himself at the fire.*

55 *And the chief priests and all the council sought for witness against Jesus to put him to death; and found none.*

56 *For many bare false witness against him, but their witness agreed not together.*

57 *And there arose certain, and bare false witness against him, saying,*

58 *We heard him say, I will destroy this temple that is made with hands, and within three days I will build another made without hands.*

59 *But neither so did their witness agree together.*

60 *And the high priest stood up in the midst, and asked Jesus, saying, Answerest thou nothing? what is it which these witness against thee?*

61 *But he held his peace, and answered nothing. Again the high priest asked him, and said unto him, Art thou the Christ, the Son of the Blessed?*

62 *And Jesus said, I am: and ye shall see the Son of man sitting on the right hand of power, and coming in the clouds of heaven.*

63 *Then the high priest rent his clothes, and saith, What need we any further witnesses?*

64 Ye have heard the blasphemy: what think ye? And they all condemned him to be guilty of death.

65 And some began to spit on him, and to cover his face, and to buffet him, and to say unto him, Prophesy: and the servants did strike him with the palms of their hands.

66 And as Peter was beneath in the palace, there cometh one of the maids of the high priest:

67 And when she saw Peter warming himself, she looked upon him, and said, And thou also wast with Jesus of Nazareth.

68 But he denied, saying, I know not, neither understand I what thou sayest. And he went out into the porch; and the cock crew.

69 And a maid saw him again, and began to say to them that stood by, This is one of them.

70 And he denied it again. And a little after, they that stood by said again to Peter, Surely thou art one of them: for thou art a Galilaean, and thy speech agreeth thereto.

71 But he began to curse and to swear, saying, I know not this man of whom ye speak.

72 And the second time the cock crew. And Peter called to mind the word that Jesus said unto him, Before the cock crow twice, thou shalt deny me thrice. And when he thought thereon, he wept.

CHAPTER 40

Late that night, Tracilla was visited by Kasha and her husband. The young couple came into a home devoid of any emotion, with Tracilla sitting in the corner of the room rocking back and forth in her self imposed misery. She was treated as an inanimate object by everyone in the house. They simply ignored her and went about their business of living. Kasha was shocked at the appearance of Tracilla. She seemed to have aged ten years since Kasha had last seen her. The misery of her life was written all over her face and body. She was immobilized by fear and dared not speak unless spoken to.

Kasha wrapped her arms around her bereaved friend to give her some type of physical comfort. Kasha's husband began to explain to Micah the reason for their late night visit. They had just received word that the Man of Galilee had been secretly arrested by the religious leaders. Kasha continued to comfort her friend as the enormity of what had happened began to sink into Tracilla's very soul. She began to wail in misery as Kasha's husband explained that the gentle man had been spit upon, beaten by the soldiers and then condemned to death for blasphemy by the High Priest.

Tracilla, in a small way, actually felt the loneliness the savior was feeling when Kasha explained how everyone had deserted him during and after the arrest. Even Peter, who swore he would never desert him, was bereft because he had openly denied Jesus before the people who were gathered outside of the temple.

Kasha took Tracilla by the shoulders and gently made her look at her in the face. "Now is the time, Tracilla, you can not wait any longer. You will live this way for the rest of your life if you do not seek this man's forgiveness. From the bottom of my soul, I know it is imperative you speak with him somehow. You must bear your soul to him before it is too late. Tracilla, look at me, do not turn away! I know the message of Jesus has pierced your heart, yet your pride keeps you from receiving his wonderful gift of forgiveness. In all of his words, he has said over and over how this gift is for everyone who repents and asks for it. Tracilla, time is short. They are planning to kill the Savior as soon as they can. You must try and speak with him. You must show him how sorrowful you are for all the destruction you have caused."

Tracilla's heart was breaking as she realized time was very short. She did not know what to do. She knew the answer could be found in Jesus, yet still she felt what she had done was unforgivable. How could he forgive her, when what she had done was openly try to bring about the very thing that was happening? She had betrayed her husband, her children, her friends, and even her faith. How could there be forgiveness for such things?

As she wept, Kasha held her, while Micah looked at her with disgust. Kasha looked around at the devastation brought about by the wickedness of the tongue and even she, in her newfound faith, saw no possible healing. Yet something within her pushed at her to take Tracilla home, to stand by her and show her the way. Kasha's compassion was only matched by the animosity shown by Micah.

Unable to restrain himself anymore, Micah looked at Tracilla and raged, "Why are you crying, Woman? This is what you wanted. You should be dancing around in joy. You have been a part of the destruction of another human being. Wasn't this your ultimate goal? Woman, you disgust me. I can see now our whole home has been built on your lies and deception. That is the reason it is all falling apart. It is because of you and your insatiable need for wickedness. I can even see now that Ashon is better off where she is than to be here with you. May God forgive me for the hate I hold for you!"

Kasha recoiled at the venom coming from Tracilla's husband. "How could he be so cruel? Couldn't he see the misery in Tracilla over what was happening? Tracilla would never find the truth in this house. "She must go with me", Kasha thought. Kasha took her husband aside to ask his permission to carry Tracilla home with them. He readily agreed as he was appalled at the hostile treatment she was receiving. Even though he had never cared for Kasha's association with the woman, he could not see treating anyone as she was being treated.

Kasha went to Tracilla's room, which was now the smallest in the house, and packed for her. When Kasha told Micah what she planned to do, she saw a look of relief come over him. He was relieved to be free of the burden Tracilla had become. He did not even ask when she would return. He just told Kasha, "Take her!" As Tracilla left, there was not a word spoken or even a gesture of farewell lifted toward the once stately woman. She quietly left the house not knowing if she would ever return or see her family again.

Kasha and Mark practically carried Tracilla through the streets to their home. It was very late, yet some people who heard Tracilla's cries looked out to see what was causing such a sound. It must have been a very strange sight to see the young couple carrying the person who had become the joke of the land. Maybe if they had been carrying someone else, people would have stopped the couple and asked what was happening? Because of who they were helping, most people merely shrugged their shoulders and grinned secretly, glad Tracilla had finally gotten her just rewards.

One witness rushed to Patisha's home to tell her what they had seen. Patisha had a great laugh at the thought of how crazy her former friend must have seemed. While Patisha and her visitor were having a great laugh, Mark and Kasha put Tracilla to bed, staying up throughout the night trying to figure out what they could do for Tracilla. They both agreed her state of mind was a result of the many sins she had heaped upon herself because of her wicked deeds. Restoration would only come if she repented and felt the forgiveness of a loving God. They had seen enough miracles and been under enough of the Master's teachings, to know this forgiveness could only be found in the One and Only Son of God. They also knew his stay on this earth was coming to an end. They felt desperate. They knew Tracilla needed the forgiveness of this man before his death, yet they did not know how she would be able to get it. Mark and Kasha began to pray in unison for the Lord to open up doors to make this possible.

While Mark and Kasha were praying for Tracilla, Patisha joined her husband in bed after her late night visitor. Still laughing about what she had been told, Patisha's husband wanted to know what caused her such mirth. Patisha began to tell her husband about the scene Tracilla had caused in the streets. As she was telling him, she inadvertently mentioned about the scene at the council when Tracilla had given her dramatic litany. Patisha's husband immediately grew very angry because he realized his own wife had been a part of Tracilla's scandalous accusations against Jesus.

He told Patisha to get dressed as she was going to go to Micah and this man Jesus and beg forgiveness. Patisha cried out in misery over the curse of her loose lips.

They traveled to Micah's house and awoke the household. Patisha told the complete story and pleaded with Micah to forgive her and Tracilla for their treachery. She begged Micah to go to Tracilla and reason with her. Micah remained stoneface during the long, late night conversation. In the early morning hours, something was awakened in Micah, a need to go to Jesus before it was too late. The urge was so strong he immediately left with Patisha and her husband to travel to Jerusalem. Not once did they complain about their tired bodies. This urgency grew more powerful with each step they took.

CHAPTER 41

Very early in the morning, the chief priests, with the elders, the teachers of the law and the whole Sanhedrin, reached a decision. They bound Jesus, led him away and handed him over to Pilate.

"Are you the king of the Jews?" asked Pilate.

"Yes, it is as you say," Jesus replied.

The chief priests accused him of many things. So again Pilate asked him, "Aren't you going to answer? See how many things they are accusing you of."

But Jesus Still made no reply, and Pilate was amazed.

Mark, Kasha and Tracilla had made the trip in remarkable time. Mark was amazed at how time seemed to stand still. When they entered the city, they saw the crowds of people going toward Pilate's palace. They followed the crowd. Tracilla could hear people talking about the Nazarene. The things she heard made her stomach turn. The people were all talking about his lowly birth, his mother's supposed indiscretion and how he was a fraud. That the King of the Jews would never be born to such lowly people. These were the things Tracilla had spoken that day by the Jordan River. Her spark of malice had grown to a crescendo of self righteous judgment. As she walked among the crowd she continually told the people what they were saying was untrue. But the fire had grown too large for any single person to stop as it raged from flaming tongue to the next.

Now it was the custom of the Feast to release a prisoner whom the people requested. A man called Barabbas was in prison with the insurrectionists who had committed murder in the uprising. The crowd came up and asked Pilate to do for them what he usually did.

"Do you want me to release to you the king of the Jews?" asked Pilate, knowing it was out of envy that the chief priests had handed Jesus over to him. But the chief priests stirred up the crowd to have Pilate release Barabbas instead.

The crowds cried to release Barabbas. The chief priests were amazed at how easily it was to get the crowd to agree with them. They didn't realized how it had all been set in motion years before.

"What shall I do, then, with the one you call the king of the Jews?" Pilate asked them.

"Crucify him!" they shouted.

"Why? What crime has he committed?" asked Pilate.

But they shouted all the louder. "Crucify him!"

Wanting to satisfy the crowd, Pilate released Barabbas to them. He had Jesus flogged, and handed him over to be crucified.

Mark, Kasha and Tracilla were horrified when they heard the verdict. Pilate had let the people decide the fate of Jesus. The man of Galilee was to be crucified, not for any crime he had committed, but for the crime of the people who were so susceptible to rumor and innuendo. Mark and Kasha wanted to leave, but Tracilla insisted they stay. She wanted to make one last attempt to let this good man know she was so sorry for what she had done. She did not know how, she only knew she must.

The soldiers led Jesus away into the palace (that is, the Praetorium) and called together the whole company of soldiers. They put a purple robe on him, then twisted together a crown of thorns and set it on him. And they began to call out to him. "Hail, king of the Jews!" Again and again they struck him on the head with a staff and spit on him. Falling on their knees, they paid homage to him. And when they had mocked him, they took off the purple robe and put his own clothes on him. Then they led him out to crucify him.

Tracilla ran down the streets looking for a place to stand where she might be near the Savior as he came down the streets with his cross. Mark and Kasha followed behind afraid for their friend and her urgency to get near the Savior. Miraculously there was a small opening in the crowd on the main road leading to a place called Golgotha. Tracilla stood by the street and watched for her opportunity.

As the crowd cheered and mocked Jesus, he carried his cross down the road. Weakened from the beatings and the trauma of all that was happening to him, he faltered many times. At one point he drew a deep breath and became faint. The weight of the cross pushed him toward the side of the street. When he stumbled, he slowly arose to come face to face with one of his greatest enemies.

Tracilla's face was red and swollen from all of her crying. Her sobs took on an inhuman sound as she looked at the bruised and bleeding face of "The Christ." His clear eyes looked at her, not with the hate she deserved, but with the love she was seeking. Having only moments to tell him, she opened her mouth to say, "I am sorry!" Crying had taken away her voice. She tried to say the words so the Savior could hear them over the roaring crowds. It was impossible, yet Jesus, through his blood and sweat, whispered the words she so longed to hear, "I forgive you, Tracilla, go and sin no more." He had seen into her heart and had seen the repentance. The words she tried to speak with her mouth were heard by the Savior from her heart.

At this point, a certain man from Cyrene, Simon, the father of Alexander and Rufus, was passing by on his way in from the country, and they forced him to carry the cross. They brought Jesus to the place called Golgotha (which means the Place of the Skull). Then they offered him wine mixed with myrrh, but he did not take it. And they crucified him. Dividing up his clothes, they cast lots to see what each would get.

It was the third hour when they crucified him. The written notice of the charge against him read: THE KING OF THE JEWS. They crucified two robbers with him, one on his right and one on his left. Those who passed by hurled insults at him, shaking their heads and saying, "So! You who are going to destroy the temple and build it in three days, come down from the cross and save yourself!"

In the same way the chief priests and the teachers of the law mocked him among themselves. "He saved others," they said, "but he can't save himself! Let this Christ, this King of Israel, come down now from the cross, that we may see and believe." Those crucified with him also heaped insults on him.

At the sixth hour darkness came over the whole land until the ninth hour. And at the ninth hour Jesus cried out in a loud voice, "Eloi, Eloi, lama sabachthani?" which means, "My God, my God, why have you forsaken me?"

When some of those standing near heard this, they said, "Listen, he's calling Elijah."

One man ran, filled a sponge with wine vinegar, put it on a stick, and offered it to Jesus to drink. "Now leave him alone. Let's see if Elijah comes to take him down," he said.

With a loud cry, Jesus breathed his last.

The curtain of the temple was torn in two from top to bottom. And when the centurion, who stood there in front of Jesus, heard his cry and saw how he died, he said, "Surely this man was the Son of God!"

Some women were watching from a distance. Among them were Mary Magdalene, Mary the mother of James the younger and of Joses, and Salome. In Galilee these women had followed him and cared for his needs. Many other women who had come up with him to Jerusalem were also there.

An unknown woman of grand countenance stood among them. With an air of authority, she pronounced, "It was inevitable this would happen, he was a man born of lowly means. He could not possibly dream he could change the world." A strange thing happened. Instead of rushing to hear more, the women quietly turned and left the woman of influence. Her whisper would only be heard with her own ears.

Proverbs 6:16-19 King James Version (KJV)

*16 These six things doth the L*ORD *hate: yea, seven are an abomination unto him:*

17 A proud look, a lying tongue, and hands that shed innocent blood,

18 An heart that deviseth wicked imaginations, feet that be swift in running to mischief,

19 A false witness that speaketh lies, and he that soweth discord among brethren.

Printed in the United States
By Bookmasters